The Carradignes: American Royalty

Who's Who?

Prince Jace Carradigne: Sure, he's the king of his own cell-phone empire, but who knew that Jace was actually an heir to a throne! And now he's found the woman of his dreams. But all is not happily-ever-after in Jace's fairy-tale world....

Victoria Meadland: This charming cocktail waitress has always done for herself until her very own Prince Charming sweeps her off her feet. But Victoria has a secret that may keep her from becoming a real-life Cinderella.

Prince Markus Carradigne: The Korosolan throne should have been his. And this disinherited prince is prepared to use any means necessary to ensure that he, not Jace, receives the crown.

King Easton Carradigne: This noble ruler won't rest until he finds the right man—or woman—to succeed him.

Dear Reader,

Millionaire. Prince. Secret agent. Doctor. If any—or all—of these men strike your fancy, well…you're in luck! These fabulous guys are waiting for you in the pages of this month's offerings from Harlequin American Romance.

His best friend's request to father her child leads millionaire Gabe Deveraux to offer a bold marriage proposal in *My Secret Wife* by Cathy Gillen Thacker, the latest installment of THE DEVERAUX LEGACY series. A royal request makes Prince Jace Carradigne heir to a throne—and in search of his missing fiancée—in Mindy Neff's *The Inconveniently Engaged Prince*, part of our ongoing series THE CARRADIGNES: AMERICAN ROYALTY. (And there are royals galore to be found when the series comes to a sensational ending in *Heir to the Throne*, a special two-in-one collection by Kasey Michaels and Carolyn Davidson, available next month wherever Harlequin books are sold.)

Kids, kangaroos and a kindhearted woman are all in a day's work for cool and collected secret agent Mike Wheeler in *Secret Service Dad*, the second book in Mollie Molay's GROOMS IN UNIFORM series. And a big-city doctor attempts to hide his true identity—and his affections—for a Montana beauty in *The Doctor Wore Boots* by Debra Webb, the conclusion to the TRADING PLACES duo.

So be sure to catch all of these wonderful men this month—and every month—as you enjoy their wonderful love stories from Harlequin American Romance.

Happy reading,

Melissa Jeglinski
Associate Senior Editor
Harlequin American Romance

THE INCONVENIENTLY ENGAGED PRINCE

Mindy Neff

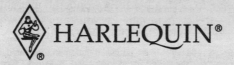

HARLEQUIN®

TORONTO • NEW YORK • LONDON
AMSTERDAM • PARIS • SYDNEY • HAMBURG
STOCKHOLM • ATHENS • TOKYO • MILAN • MADRID
PRAGUE • WARSAW • BUDAPEST • AUCKLAND

Special thanks and acknowledgment are given to
Mindy Neff for her contribution to
THE CARRADIGNES: AMERICAN ROYALTY.

To Michelle Thorne,
Super heroine and proprietress of the
fabulous Bearly Used Books store.
You're a classy, gracious and fun lady,
and the best kind of friend!

ISBN 0-373-16946-9

THE INCONVENIENTLY ENGAGED PRINCE

ABOUT THE AUTHOR

Mindy Neff published her first book with Harlequin American Romance in 1995. Since then, she has appeared regularly on the Waldenbooks bestseller list and won numerous awards, including the National Readers' Choice Award, the *Romantic Times* Career Achievement Award, three W.I.S.H. Awards for Outstanding Hero and two Gold Medal reviews from *Romantic Times* magazine, as well as nominations for the Holt Medallion, Golden Quill, Orange Rose and twice for the prestigious RITA® Award.

Originally from Louisiana, Mindy settled in Southern California, where she married a really romantic guy and raised five great kids. Family, friends, writing and reading are her passions. When Mindy is not writing, her ideal getaway is a good book, hot sunshine and a chair at the river's edge at her second home in Parker, Arizona.

Mindy loves to hear from readers. You can write to her at 8502 E. Chapman, #355, Orange, CA 92869, or through her Web site at www.mindyneff.com, or e-mail at mindyneff@aol.com.

Books by Mindy Neff

*Tall, Dark & Irresistible
†Bachelors of Shotgun Ridge

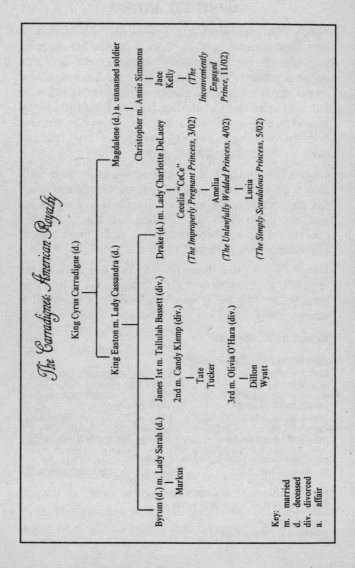

The Carradignes: American Royalty

King Cyrus Carradigne (d.)

King Easton m. Lady Cassandra (d.)

Magdalene (d.) a. unnamed soldier

Christopher m. Annie Simmons

Jace
Kelly

*(The
Inconveniently
Engaged
Prince, 11/02)*

Byrum (d.) m. Lady Sarah (d.)

Markus

James 1st m. Tallulah Bassett (div.)

2nd m. Candy Klemp (div.)

Tate
Tucker

3rd m. Olivia O'Hara (div.)

Dillon
Wyatt

Drake (d.) m. Lady Charlotte DeLacey

Cecelia "CeCe"

(The Improperly Pregnant Princess, 3/02)

Amelia

(The Unlawfully Wedded Princess, 4/02)

Lucia

(The Simply Scandalous Princess, 5/02)

Key:
m.   married
d.   deceased
div.   divorced
a.   affair

Prologue

He was surrounded by luxury, the best money could buy, but this particular October in Manhattan was damned cold. He paced the richly decorated rooms of his midtown apartment, ice tinkling in his tumbler of scotch—the finest brand, of course.

When his private phone rang, he didn't immediately answer, hoped to God that idiot he was spending a king's ransom on would remember to use the code.

After three rings, he punched the call button. "Speak."

"Jace Carradigne's clean. One speeding ticket four years ago. That's it."

"Not good enough. You know what I need." He gulped scotch, desperate to feel the buzz. The buzz sharpened his mind, calmed him.

"Yes, of course. It might take some time, though. His company's telecommunication stock is due to split—for the third time. His employees regard him as a pal. He can name his own hours or take a five-year sabbatical and never have to alter his lifestyle. The guy's rolling in dough.''

His fingers tightened around the crystal tumbler in his hand, the pressure threatening to shatter the heavy, obnoxiously expensive glass. Why did everyone else get these lucky breaks?

Money and power should be *his*. It was his *right*.

And the old man wanted to take it away from him.

It's not going to happen. If he couldn't find the information he needed to discredit Jace Carradigne, he'd just have to do it the hard way.

He sipped his scotch, letting the smooth fire dance on his tongue. Truthfully, arranging...*accidents* wasn't as difficult as most people believed. And pointing the finger away from himself was like taking candy from a baby.

He nearly giggled at the rush of power that swam through the pleasant haze of alcohol. Let anyone dare to get in his way and they'd suffer the consequences. He just had to let them *know* they were getting in his way.

After that...well, forewarned was being sporting on his part. He wondered if Jace Carradigne liked to play.

''You have one week. Either get me something, or you're out.''

Chapter One

Victoria Meadland's stomach cartwheeled as she looked up and saw him crossing the crowded bar.

Jace Carradigne had been coming to the trendy nightclub in San Diego's Gaslamp Quarter every Friday evening with his pals for several months now.

Recently, he'd been coming in more often. And alone.

To see her.

Her fingers trembled against the tray of dirty glasses and half-empty beer bottles she was in the process of dumping. She cleared her tray and handed the bartender, Paul, the next round of orders she'd collected.

Diamond Jim's did an excellent business on most any night of the week, but Fridays were the busiest. She only worked part-time, but she needed the job until she could get her final college credits and start teaching school, which was her real dream.

And that meant she shouldn't be fraternizing with the customers. Or anticipating a certain man's contagious smile or exuberant compliments.

The problem was, Jace's appearance was something she'd come to count on, to look for. It was like a standing date that neither of them had actually agreed to. Every time she saw him, she wanted to pinch herself.

Tall and surfer-guy handsome, his skin tanned, his dark blond hair streaked from the California sun, he headed straight toward her, made her feel as though she'd stepped into the pages of a fairy tale.

He always had a ready smile on his face and was quick to laugh or tease. His dynamic personality simply swept others along in his powerful presence.

She cautioned herself to be careful. God knows she'd made enough mistakes in her life. She wasn't going to jump so fast this time. No matter what her heart bade her otherwise.

She swept her shoulder-length brown hair behind her ear and tried to still the pounding of her heart. Jazz music vied with the raised voices of couples, tourists and business pals unwinding after the workweek. For an instant, everything seemed to fade into the background, as though a friendly sorceress or angel had snapped the world into freeze mode.

Jace eased up to the bar, a dimple creasing his cheek, his hair tousled from the late October evening breeze.

"I swear I've never seen a prettier sight. Marry me, Victoria."

She nearly choked on her breath. The din of music and voices swirled into the forefront of her consciousness once more.

For one heart-stopping moment, she almost imagined he was serious. Then she got a grip.

She shook her head. "Jace, Jace. You know I can't do that."

"Sure you can. Say yes and I'll have the company plane wing us over to Vegas."

"And be responsible for hearts breaking all over Southern California? Sorry, pal. Too much burden for my conscience." This wasn't the first time he'd greeted her with the outrageous suggestion.

"I already told you. I'm free as a bird. Not a single heart on the line for you to worry about."

"You might be surprised," she murmured. Her own heart was straddling a precarious line.

"What was that?"

"Nothing." She wiped away a circle of water on the bar and refilled the bowl of popcorn.

"Hmm." The twinkle in his eye said he didn't believe her, but would let it go for the moment. "Since I've asked you to marry me, don't you think you should at least agree to go out with me?"

"You're crazy," she said, half-amused, more than a little tempted.

"About you."

Lord, he was cute. Funny, attentive, wealthy… "You don't even know me."

"Sure I do. I've seen you at least once a week for the past month. That makes us practically engaged." He checked his watch. "You're off in half an hour, right? Let me take you out for a late dinner."

"I have to study."

"No one should study on an empty stomach. It's a Carradigne rule."

She bit her lip to keep from laughing. "I already had dinner."

"What, at five o'clock? That was almost six hours ago. Okay, how about coffee? Come on, Vickie. Say yes."

She picked up the tray Paul had filled with the latest drink order and scooted out from behind the bar. Passing his stool, she hesitated for a fraction of an instant. The darn man was simply too irresistible.

"Yes."

He whooped and she hid a grin as she made her way through tables filled with patrons, several of which shouldn't be ordering another alcoholic beverage. The saxophone player on stage announced this was the last song of the set and rattled off the dates and places where their group would be appearing next.

As she delivered drinks and stuffed tips in her pocket, she kept a subtle eye on Jace Carradigne. More than one female in the room tried to get his attention, but he didn't seem to notice. Instead, his gaze followed her as though she were the only woman in the universe.

It was a heady experience. Especially for Victoria. A man like Jace Carradigne seemed too good to be true. Then again, she might be building fantasies where they didn't belong. She hadn't even had a formal date with him.

Yet.

Why had she agreed to go out with him tonight after

refusing him for the past month? She'd thought he'd lose interest after the first couple of times she'd said no. She was sure he was just teasing, being friendly, passing a Friday night. Being a flirt.

But there was something deeper in his laughing green eyes. Something that made her want to ease into him and let him slay her dragons and be her knight.

And those kind of thoughts were ones that would get her in trouble. She had plenty of past experience to go by. From now on, she was going to look before she leapt. She wasn't going to try to define herself through a man. Wasn't going to search for love in all the wrong places, or mistake infatuation for the real thing.

Been there, done that, she thought, unconsciously touching the two sapphire rings she wore on the middle finger of her right hand. And the consequences had left irreparable scars on her soul.

"Looks like you've made Mr. Cell Phone millionaire a happy man," Tiffany Hershey commented as she scooted Vickie aside and automatically began clearing dirty glasses from the table.

"Why do you always define people by their profession or bank account?"

Tiffany shrugged and grinned. "Girl, bank accounts are important. And when they come with a guy who looks like that…" Her gaze strayed toward the bar. "Well, I'd say you've struck the mother lode."

"There's more to Jace than his business success," Vickie defended.

"Mmm, and you're going to find out how much more, right?"

"We're just going for coffee."

"I know. I overheard. And you were officially off the clock three minutes ago." Tiffany laid a hand on Vickie's arm, her heavily made-up eyes turning serious. "Give him a chance, hon."

"Tiffany…"

"Don't give me that tone. You've got a wall around you a mile high. All you do is work and study. You deserve some happiness in your life."

Over one too many glasses of wine after work one night, Vickie had told Tiffany about her life and the reason she'd sworn off men. She didn't often tell her secrets to others, and had regretted opening up to the other woman. Just thinking about it brought her shame.

But Tiffany had turned out to be a gentle champion and confidante. Despite the other woman's flamboyance, they'd formed a friendship.

"He's out of my league."

"Get outta here. You've got more to offer a man than most of them even deserve. Sometimes I think you're too sweet for your own good, but I think this guy's different. He doesn't strike me as one to take advantage."

"If he is, he won't get far with me. I'm not traveling that road again."

"That's a great attitude, hon. But you still have to bend a little. Let people in."

"We'll see." She'd let people in before. Too easily.

And the bones of the myriad skeletons in her closet were a rattling echo in her heart and mind. Every day.

The bar would be open for another three hours, but like Tiffany had pointed out, Vickie's shift was over. She retrieved her tips for the night and slipped in the back room to hang up her apron and grab her denim jacket. Paul was good about working around her school schedule, letting her have flexible hours and plenty of time to study.

At thirty-one, she was starting a bit late in the game toward a career, but better late than never. She was going to make something of herself. Securing an education and a stable, respectable career as a teacher meant everything to her. Eventually, she might even pursue her master's and go into counseling.

She'd long ago lost contact with any of the people from the group homes she was raised in, but it was a burning point of pride that she show them—at least in her own mind—that she could excel, overcome the sins of the past.

A past where nobody had cared enough to ask if a little girl had dreams.

As a teacher, perhaps she could make a difference in just one child's life. Be the type of role model she'd always wished had been there for her. Help a young girl or boy realize that they could reach for a dream.

Her heart thumped in her chest and her nerve endings tingled as she headed back to the counter where Jace Carradigne sipped a beer and waited for her. She wasn't afraid of the man himself. She was afraid of what he made her feel. What he could easily make her forget: that she'd sworn off relationships until she'd graduated from college and accomplished her teaching goals.

He stood when she approached. "Ready?"

"I really should go home and study. I've got a psychology test on Monday."

"See there? You're in luck. I'm the perfect guy to help you out in that area."

A bubble of laughter tickled its way up her throat. "I'm afraid to ask how."

"I excelled in psychology classes in college. Had to actually, just to save my sanity. You see my sister, Kelly, was one of those gifted kids. She's only twenty-six, but she's already a scientist. She's got multiple degrees in various fields of medicine."

"And why did that compel you to study psychology?" They made their way toward the door and Vickie waved good-night to Tiffany.

"Because she used bigger words than I could understand."

Vickie rolled her eyes. "I doubt that. According to your friends who've so helpfully given you references, you're a self-made success story. The king of cell phones. A man like that's not intimidated by a few big words."

"See? Great guys, my friends. The king title's a little over the top—even though I am related to a royal family. Was it my buddies singing my praises that made you decide to go out with me?"

She wanted to smile at the way he teasingly claimed a connection to royalty. She knew he'd deliberately put his friends up to giving him "references." And they'd had great fun doing it. "I haven't really decided to go out with you."

"Too late. We're out." He gestured around to the crisp night where quaint wrought iron streetlamps illuminated the sidewalks in front of restored buildings that had stood since the 1870s. "And you're with me."

She shook her head. "Literal, aren't you?"

"I can be. Think of me as your study aid. We'll exchange information, delve into each other's psyche. I'm an open book. Anything you want to know, just ask."

Hiking the strap of her purse over her shoulder, she shoved her hands in the pockets of her denim jacket. The October air was brisk and invigorating. "Are you always so…"

"So what?"

"I don't know. Happy?"

He laughed. "It's called being positive. It's an energy. Very effective business tool."

"And personal one as well."

"Is it working?"

"I think you know it is." She glanced at the sidewalk tables outside a café. "Where are we going, anyway?"

"Well, it's your call, but I've got a great condo across the bay. Incredible view. And I make a killer omelet. Decent coffee, too."

"And I suppose you have some etchings you'd like to show me, as well?"

He slapped a wide palm to his chest. "Victoria, my love. You wound me. I'm a perfect gentleman."

She couldn't help but laugh. The man inspired it. He also made her nervous. Especially when he used those endearments so casually. "I think I'm a little overwhelmed by you."

"Can't have that. We'll save the view for next time. How about the coffee shop around the corner. They've got a great caramel apple pie."

"Now that's just flat-out not fair. I'm a sweets nut."

He leaned in close. "Mmm. I figured that about you. Will it scare you off if I warn you I'm dying to take a bite?" His eyes caressed her hair, her lips. "Of you."

Desire washed over her so swiftly her head swam. Not good. *Don't backslide, Vickie.*

She cleared her throat, took her hands out of her pockets and fiddled with the strap of her purse. "Um…yes."

"Okay. We'll ease into that."

"Jace—"

He paused, put a finger over her lips. "You're safe with me, Victoria. I joke around a lot, but I'm a nice guy. Honest."

The warmth of his finger against her lips made her want to taste him. In his eyes was sincerity. The problem was, she'd been taken in before. She wasn't too sure about her own judgment when it came to men and their intentions.

Oh, she wanted to believe him. Wanted to let down her guard and be a normal woman who could take life as it came and not worry about appearances or mistakes or anything else. But the past was always there. Lurking. A reminder.

"You're thinking too hard," he said.

"I'm a little rusty at this sort of thing."

"What, going for coffee? It's a snap. Just follow my lead."

Just like that he could put her at ease. She decided he was right. She *was* thinking this to death. For once in a very long time, she was going to go with the flow and simply relax in the company of a nice man.

"Then lead on."

JACE CHOSE a corner booth at a trendy coffee house, and watched as Vickie slid onto the sea-green, vinyl bench. He wanted to scoot in next to her, feel the warmth of her body against his, but sat opposite her instead. He didn't want to scare her off when she'd finally agreed to come out with him.

It was crazy really. He'd never reacted this way to a woman before. But the moment he'd seen her serving drinks at Diamond Jim's he'd been hooked. Maybe it was the innocence of her sweet smile, or the dimples in her cheeks, or the soft music of her voice, or that intriguing glimpse of the little tattoo he'd seen on the small of her back when her sweater had ridden up as she'd bent over to wipe a table.

Or maybe it was something deeper. She touched him on a level he couldn't quite define.

He didn't know her, but wanted to remedy that. She was beautiful in a wholesome way, fresh and intriguing. She didn't give much away, and he'd tried like mad to get her to open up. Instead, like a woman of mystery, she'd just smile and glide away—intriguing him all the more.

He'd teasingly gotten his friends to vouch for him and found himself suddenly nervous over her opinion. What had started as a friendly lark, a flirtation with a pretty waitress, had become soul-deep important.

He watched as she tucked her mink-colored hair behind her ears. He'd come to know the gesture as a nervous one.

What he was experiencing was more like a gut instinct—an incredibly *strong* gut instinct. And he'd made millions in the business world relying on his hunches.

He had an idea Victoria Meadland was going to change his life.

"Relax," he said.

"I told you, I'm out of practice."

"There are no expectations, here. I'd like it if we could just be ourselves."

"Is that a rarity in your business life?"

He shrugged. "Not really. I'm the kind of guy who figures you might as well take me as I come."

"I admire that kind of self-confidence."

"Anybody can have it. In fact, I give miniseminars on positive attitudes to my employees. It's amazing what it does for closing a deal."

"Maybe I ought to sign up for one of your classes."

"Are you kidding? You could probably *teach* the class. After watching you this past month, I'd say you've got more self-confidence than my whole company put together.'' For some reason that caused her eyes to light with pleasure. Hmm. Had someone told her she wasn't good enough sometime in her life? In his book, that was inexcusable.

''It's called giving the customer what they want without letting them step over the line,'' she said.

''Like holding me at bay for over a month?''

She grinned. ''Something like that.''

The waitress stopped by their table. Jace hadn't even looked at the menu. He wasn't really hungry, but apple caramel pie was almost as much of a temptation as Vickie was.

''Did you guys want to order something?'' the waitress asked. She was young and looked like she'd rather be anywhere else but here.

Jace grinned at her, and noted that she perked up a bit. ''Absolutely. I'll have the specialty pie and a cappuccino with extra cream. Vic?''

''Cheesecake, I think. And a decaf, white chocolate latte.''

The waitress scribbled the orders and left. ''Decaf?'' he asked. ''I thought you were going to study.''

''I will. But I don't intend to be up all night doing it. What's your excuse?''

''Caffeine doesn't keep me awake.''

''Lucky you.''

''Sometimes. So, Victoria Meadland, tell me all about yourself.'' The withdrawal was subtle, but he noticed it, noticed the slight flush of her skin, as though he'd put her on the spot. He decided to change directions. "Wait. We were supposed to be studying psychology, weren't we?"

She smiled, relaxed a bit. "I don't think discussing our life stories is going to help me on the exam."

"I can use big words if it'll help."

She laughed and he sat, transfixed. She had a wonderful laugh that lit her face and eased the little worry lines between her brows.

"No?" he said when she just shook her head. He liked that she was easing into his company. "So, what are you majoring in?"

"Human development and English. I want to be a teacher. I have one more semester before I'll get my B.A. degree. Then another year to get my teaching credential."

"You can teach without the credentials, though, can't you?"

"For a while, yes. And I will, but I'll also keep up my education and go for my master's degree. That way I could go into counseling."

"You'd be good at it."

"What makes you think that?"

"I've watched you at Diamond Jim's. You've got a special way of giving the person you're talking to your complete attention. That's a good quality for a potential counselor."

"Thanks."

"So how come you didn't just major in education?"

"California doesn't offer it."

The waitress brought their coffee and dessert.

Vickie picked up her fork and took a bite of cheesecake.

Jace's mouth watered as he watched her eyes close, watched the pure, unadulterated pleasure wash across her face. "Good?"

Her eyes opened, locked onto his. "Delicious."

He was sweating. Desire streaked through him and howled for action or release. For the longest time, their eyes held. Then she glanced down as though she had just realized the sizzle and was embarrassed by it.

"Um…" She stopped, cleared her throat. "How about you? Where did you go to school."

He tasted his own pie, but even though it was excellent, it didn't compare to the look that had come over Victoria's face only moments ago. He imagined she'd wear that same expression in the throes of passion. "Virginia Tech."

"Virginia? Is that where you're from?"

"Nope. Born and raised right here in San Diego. But I knew I wanted to capitalize on the cellular telephone industry and at the time, Virginia Tech offered the best courses on wireless technology."

She laid down her fork, gave him her full attention. "How long was it before you started your company?"

"Right out of college. I built Carracell Inc. from the ground up and surrounded myself with a great group of co-workers. That was almost ten years ago, when the cellular business was really starting to boom. Seems I was at the right place at the right time."

"I imagine you put plenty of hard work into it."

"Sure. But working at something I love is like taking a vacation every day."

She sighed. "That's so neat. Especially that you figured out what you wanted to do and were able to accomplish it while you were young."

He frowned, realizing she was comparing herself to him. "You're not exactly old. What are you, twenty-five?"

She laughed. "That's the nicest compliment I've had in a while. I'm thirty-one. And attending college when you're over thirty can be a humbling, aging experience."

"Or keep you young at heart."

"That, too."

"Can I ask what made you wait to go to college? You seem pretty determined in knowing what you want."

She shifted against the vinyl seat, scooted her coffee mug back and forth across the crimson tabletop. Then she looked him square in the eye, her chin lifted as though she expected someone to take a jab.

"I ran away from a group home when I was sixteen, which meant dropping out of high school. Since I was on my own, I had to work to support myself. Then I had to get my GED and build up a cushion of funds. I was young and didn't realize I could work *and* go to college."

"It's a heavy load."

"But it'll be worth it."

He shouldn't ask about the group home. It was none of his business. But he seemed to have an insatiable need to find out everything about her. And coming from a close, happy family, the idea of not living within that circle of safety was unthinkable.

"This…uh, group home. Was it like a foster family?"

"No." She twisted the two rings on her middle finger. "I lived in a few of those. Some of them were nice, some of them just okay. The group home was more along the lines of what you'd call an orphanage for kids not yet old enough for emancipation. It was called Helen's Home. We called it Hell's Home."

From the set of her shoulders and the dare in her eyes, it was clear she wouldn't tolerate pity. And he didn't intend to give it.

But questions could easily be misconstrued. If he had his way—which he generally did—there would be plenty of time to delve into all the facets of Victoria Meadland.

He also made a mental note to himself to check into this Helen's Home. If kids were being mistreated there, he had the connections to do something about it. And he would.

"Well, from living in Hell, you've definitely evolved into an angel."

She gave a short laugh. "You're nuts."

"About you."

"Would you stop saying stuff like that?"

"Can't seem to help it. I take one look at you and the words just tumble out."

"Did that fancy college also offer a class in smooth lines to use on your dates?"

He reached over and touched her hand, made sure he had her attention. "I don't give lines, Victoria. You'll find that my word is my bond. And I don't use my words, or my promises, lightly."

Her thumb tentatively touched his finger, then retreated. "What is it you want, Jace?" she asked, her voice so quiet it was a mere puff of breath.

"You."

She started to shake her head.

"Give me a chance. That's all I'm asking."

"I don't have time for a relationship."

"You'd be surprised how much time's available when you schedule it."

"Between working and school, my schedule's pretty full."

"I know. And I don't intend to stand in your way or keep you from your goals. All I want is *some* of your time."

"Jace—"

"You feel it, too, don't you?"

She took a deep breath, let it out and nodded. There was no coy game-playing. She knew exactly what he was asking.

"Yes. I like you a lot, Jace Carradigne. But you might find out that I'm not what you're looking for. And in that case, the risk for me is just too great."

Chapter Two

Vickie had studied until 2:00 a.m., so when her telephone rang at eight-thirty Saturday morning, she wasn't feeling very civilized.

She reached for the receiver, knocked over the alarm clock she deliberately hadn't set. "'lo?"

"Did I wake you?"

Adrenaline shot through her, bringing her straight up in the bed. She snatched at the clock, looked at the time, tried like mad to get her brain in gear.

"It's eight-thirty on Saturday morning, and I'm not exactly what you'd call a lark. What do you think?"

Jace chuckled. "Sorry. I waited as long as I could."

She settled against the pillows, wondered if she'd remembered to set the automatic brew on the coffeemaker. Sissy, who'd been curled up at the end of the bed, gave a disgusted look at having been disturbed. Vickie leaned forward and scooped the cat into her arms to soothe her.

"Don't tell me you're one of those disgustingly chipper morning people."

"Guilty."

He sounded so happily contrite, she smiled, stroking Sissy's silky fur. She'd rescued the cat when it had been a mere kitten, incensed that someone could just dump something so beautiful and sweet. Then again, she knew a bit about abandonment. Since she'd always yearned for a sister, she'd named the kitten Sissy. They'd been each other's stability for three years now.

"What are you wearing right now?"

That caught her off guard, brought her fully awake faster than a pure shot of caffeine straight through an open vein. "None of your business."

"Let me guess. A little T-shirt and a pair of those comfy shorts."

She opened her mouth, closed it, then glanced down at her men's-cut flannel pajamas adorned with little sheep and half moons. "Um, not exactly."

"Am I close?"

A smart woman would *not* play this game. Lack of coffee, she told herself, could account for fewer brain cells. "Warm. I'm…comfy." Her voice softened intimately. "No T-shirt or shorts, though."

There was a beat of silence. "Oh, man. Don't tell me you sleep in the buff."

She grinned, bit her lip. "I wouldn't dream of telling you such a thing."

He groaned. "Doesn't matter. Unfortunately for me, I have a vivid imagination. Now I'll have to go take a cold shower."

"You started it. And speaking of which, did you call me at this ungodly hour just to find out what I am, or am not wearing?'' She couldn't believe she was talking to him this way. At one time in her life, this would have been the norm. Flirting had made her feel powerful, especially when a man responded in typical fashion. But she'd changed her ways, put that behind her.

She'd come to realize that the insecure part of her had been starved for affection, and the least bit of positive attention she'd received from the opposite sex had sent her straight into infatuation. An infatuation she'd immaturely mistaken for something deeper.

Thankfully…hopefully she'd wised up. Though her behavior this morning tried to tell a different story.

Still, something about the anonymity of the telephone seemed to bring out the devil-may-care side of her.

''Actually, I called to invite you to breakfast.''

''Is that all you think about? Eating?''

His tone softened, deepened. ''No. Not all the time. Lately, I've been spending a fair amount of time thinking about that little tattoo on your back.''

She blinked, tried to recall when he might have seen it. It was a tiny bouquet of happy flowers at the small of her back, the one thing left over from her misspent youth that she absolutely loved. Cold weather clothes, though, usually kept it hidden. And she certainly hadn't peeled up her top for Jace Carradigne.

Clearing her throat, she started to speak, but he cut her off.

''Before you turn me down, breakfast comes with

an offer to study. Bring your books and we'll review together. See? No excuses.''

She glanced through the miniblinds of her apartment window. Outside the day was sunny with only a few high puffy clouds in sight. In the eucalyptus tree, a clever blue jay foraged in the bark for breakfast, bobbing his tail in apparent satisfaction before taking flight.

"I think I'm pretty well prepared for the psych test.''

"Great. Then we'll eat and go sight-seeing like tourists.''

She couldn't believe how tempting that sounded. For so long now, her life had consisted of work and school, with little time left for socializing or having fun. Oh, she could have *made* more time for socializing, but she'd been so focused, so single-minded, as though doing penance.

It suddenly struck her that she was getting tired of atoning. She was on her way toward her goals. Why couldn't she enjoy the company of an exciting man?

It didn't have to turn into a sexual thing.

Friendships between opposite sexes were normal and acceptable.

"Actually, I was planning to go bird-watching today,'' she said, absently covering Sissy's ears. Sissy would rather eat a bird than watch it.

"Come again?''

"You heard me.''

"You mean like sit out in the yard and just look?''

"The yard's good. But I like the park better. Someplace with lots of trees. I was thinking about driving over to Torrey Pines and taking a short hike.''

''To watch the birds,'' he repeated.

''It counts for science credits.''

''I see.'' He sounded a little deflated, disappointed.

She twisted the phone cord around her finger. Her heart leapt into her throat and pounded. She probably shouldn't ask, but… ''Would, um…do you want to go with me?''

''Sure. I could get into bird-watching.''

He hadn't even hesitated. She let out a breath, lectured herself not to panic. It wasn't polite to uninvite. Besides, how much trouble could she get into bird-watching?

''Okay. You can either meet me somewhere or I can stop by and pick you up on my way.''

''I can come for you.''

''Nope. It's my suggestion. I'll do the driving.''

''I've got to tell you, I'm partial to a woman who likes to take charge.''

''Don't push your luck, pal.''

He laughed. ''Okay. My condo's over the bridge on Coronado. Got a piece of paper?''

Accidentally dumping Sissy off the bed, she rummaged in the nightstand drawer and came up with a pen and a dog-eared crossword puzzle book. It seemed almost sacrilegious to write down the ritzy address in the margins of a rumpled game magazine, but it was the handiest at the moment.

He gave her several telephone numbers and a gate code, as well as detailed directions that were hardly necessary. She'd taken the ferry across to the lovely seaside suburb of Coronado several times just to soak up the ambiance—to see how the wealthier half of the world lived. So she was familiar with the area.

"See you in about an hour and a half?" she asked.

"I'll be waiting."

Hanging up the phone, she glanced down at Sissy, who was staring out of faintly annoyed iridescent blue eyes.

"What? It's only bird...I mean science studying. There's no rule that says I can't invite company."

Sissy merely licked her silky fur, as though she could see right into Vickie's soul, feel the giddy butterflies winging in her stomach.

"Just wait until you see him before you take that attitude. Then try to tell me that *you* could resist."

WITH THE TOP DOWN on her ten-year-old Chrysler convertible, Vickie drove over the spectacular two-mile bridge that connected Coronado Island to the mainland. Her hair swirled in the breeze and the brisk fall air sneaked beneath her lightweight turtleneck sweater, but she loved the freedom of driving with the top down on a beautiful sunny day.

Against the blue waters of the bay, the Hotel Del Coronado stood like a grand lady with its quirky timber facade of conical towers, cupolas, turrets, balconies and dormer windows. A distant memory flashed—herself as a young girl, watching a classic Marilyn Monroe movie that had been filmed at the hotel.

Caught up in fantasy, as girls on the bud of teen-age could, she'd imagined herself right there, strolling through the acres of polished wood and old-fashioned ambiance. She'd have worn diamonds and silk, and been the love of a handsome leading man's life.

At the time, she'd been living in a foster home in Washington, and California had seemed another world away. Yet, oddly enough, it was this hotel she'd focused on when she and Chet had run away together. They'd ended up only making it as far as Los Angeles. The pull of the hotel, though, the fantasy, had finally gotten her to San Diego…alone and much, much wiser.

She shook away those thoughts, unwilling to dwell on what couldn't be changed. Definitely unwilling to spoil such a beautiful day.

Navigating the tidily maintained streets, she located Jace's condo and punched in the gate code. The place was quite impressive, as she'd known it would be. Two stories, built in a Spanish architectural style, it sat right on the beach with a third level observation deck that would no doubt have a clear view to downtown San Diego, Mission Bay and the endless Pacific Ocean beyond.

Bicyclists whizzed down the streets dodging neighbors out for a morning jog and mothers pushing children in strollers. Parked in driveways or open garages were luxury cars and sports cars that cost the earth and made Vickie feel a little self-conscious about parking her dated Chrysler on the same block as them.

Oh, well. The classics were supposed to be an in

thing. She got out of the car, breathing in the scent of the sea and fall blooms. Pots of geraniums, mums and fluffy ferns gave the oak and leaded glass entry doors a welcoming aura.

Before she could connect her knuckles with the wood, Jace was opening the door.

"Hi," he said.

Her tongue stuck to the roof of her mouth for about three seconds. He wore a white chef's apron over a pair of jeans and a torso-hugging blue sweater. His dark blond hair was streaked light in places by the sun and sexily mussed—the result of an expensive salon cut rather than lack of a comb.

And his smile…Lord have mercy, it could render a woman speechless. Especially those dimples.

His brows rose. "Do I have spinach in my teeth?"

She snapped out of her trance. "Uh, no. Sorry."

He laughed. "Come on in."

"Why are you wearing an apron?" Like a kid gazing at a castle for the very first time, she stared in awe at the high ceilings and chandelier dripping with hundreds of sparkling crystals. A gleaming piano with a mirror-clear ebony surface drew the eye toward the cavernous living room, the wall of glass, the balcony and the sea beyond.

"I invited you to breakfast, remember?"

She finally found her manners and stopped gawking at the house, looking instead at him. "But I thought we changed the plans and decided on the park."

"Did you already eat?"

"Well, no. But—"

"Then come on in and let me impress you with my skills."

Now, *there* was an invitation that ought to make a woman wary.

She followed him across sandstone tiles and up several plush carpeted stairs to a kitchen that also boasted a wall of glass and a clear view of both the city and the sea. At night it would be even more breathtaking.

Acres of granite counters flowed over and around top-of-the-line stainless steel appliances—two of almost everything, she noted. She could probably fit her entire apartment in this one room alone.

"Um, are you trying to impress me?" *Good grief, Vickie, stop stammering!*

"Actually, yes."

"Well, at least you're honest. Can't say as much for the modesty."

He waved a spatula at her. "Told you, I'm a take-me-as-I-am kind of guy."

Yes, and she would love to take him. Because her heart was pumping like mad, she glanced away.

The dining table was set with china and crystal. Orange juice filled goblets and champagne iced in a bucket beside two of the chairs.

Something smelled absolutely wonderful. Arming himself with oven mitts, he bent and removed an egg casserole from the oven. Vickie decided that a man in close-fitting jeans wearing an apron was a dangerous combination for a woman's heart.

"How in the world did you manage to have this all catered in a little over an hour?"

He took the serving dish to the table, lowered his brows. "If I'd had it catered, do you think I'd be parading around in an apron?"

"Probably. You said you were out to impress me."

"With my winning skills, woman. I'm a great cook. Mimosa?" he asked, holding the champagne bottle over the goblet of orange juice.

She shook her head. "Not for me. I'm driving."

"You don't have to, you know."

"That was the deal. Besides, I need a clear mind and clear *vision* to see the birds."

"Good point." He put the bottle back on ice and pulled out her chair in a gentlemanly gesture that charmed her. "Breakfast is served."

She sat and waited while he retrieved a basket of croissants out of a warming oven, and took an icy bowl of fruit out of the fridge.

"Mom and dad, though they were home a lot, had demanding careers," he said as he put the rest of the meal on the table, shrugged out of his apron, and sat down. "So, I learned to cook. My sister, Kelly, was too wrapped up in her latest invention to be bothered with cooking chores. Besides, I was afraid she'd try some experiment and blow up the kitchen."

"She sounds fascinating."

"She'd be stunned to hear herself described as fascinating—although she is. Very much so." He lifted his juice glass. "Here's to our second date."

Vickie had automatically picked up her glass, but hesitated over the toast. "It's not a date."

He leaned forward and clinked the edges of the crystal. "Let a guy have his fantasies, will you?"

She chuckled and took a sip of juice. "This really does look fabulous. You didn't have to cook for me, though."

"I like to cook. It's creative and relaxing."

"That's a commonality we don't share."

"You don't cook?"

"Sure. I'm an ace with the microwave. If it comes out of the freezer and has instructions on the package, I'm right up there in a class with the Naked Chef."

"Hmm. I've seen that guy's cooking show on cable and I don't recall him ever instructing on frozen meals."

"Maybe I should write in and put it in the suggestion box."

"Maybe you should just marry me and let me cook for you."

She choked on a bite of egg and spinach soufflé. Her eyes watering, she gave him a dark look and waited for him to say, "just kidding." When he didn't, just sat there and smiled with his lips canted to the left and his dimples winking, she looked away and took a sip of water.

"Has anybody ever accused you of sounding like a broken record?"

"Mmm." He speared a cube of melon and popped it in his mouth. "Once a competitor got a little nasty at a meeting and said our cell phones sounded like a static-ridden LP album with a scratch etched in the grooves. Does that count?"

She stared at him for a full two seconds. Then she laughed. "Your mother probably spoiled you rotten as a kid, didn't she?"

"Sure. Doesn't everyone's?" The minute he said the words, she could see he wanted to take them back. "Ah, man, Vickie. I didn't mean—"

"It's okay. It's not your fault you had parents who kept you."

"I feel like a jerk."

"Don't. I love it when you laugh and clown around. And I'm not sensitive about that area of my life." Others, perhaps, but she'd come to terms with the abandonment.

"Does it bother you to talk about it?"

She shrugged. "Not much to talk about, really. I never knew who my father was. When I was about five, my mother decided she couldn't afford me anymore, so she turned me over to the state."

"When you were five?"

He was so stunned and appalled on her behalf, she wanted to reach across the table and hug him. "Yes. Old enough to remember. That was the unforgivable thing during my growing-up years. She was a drug addict. Had more boyfriends than there were days in the week. Drugs won out over maternal instincts, I guess."

"Did you ever try to look her up when you were older?"

"Yes. It's strange how we cling to hope, even when bad things happen to us. I found out that she died two years after she gave me away."

He reached for her hand. Not in pity. She could tell the difference. His touch was gentle, yet strong. The slight squeeze held compassion, yes, but mainly support.

"You've got to be proud of yourself."

"Why?"

"Because you've lived your life and made good choices when you could have dwelled on the negative and taken a different turn like so many others do."

She felt the immediate twinge of shame pour over her, twisted the rings on her finger. "All my choices haven't been so great."

"You're about to get your college degree. You work instead of standing in line for food stamps. You haven't had the support of family to back you, yet you've forged ahead. That's something to be proud of."

She wasn't used to people singing her praises. It pleased her more than she wanted to admit. Unable to find adequate words, she mumbled, "Thanks," and concentrated on the fabulous breakfast before her.

"COOL CAR," Jace said as they headed back over the bay toward town. "It suits you." He loved the way the wind twirled her silky hair.

"I like it."

He reached over and brushed a strand of hair that kept catching in her mouth. He could see her eyes from the corners of her sunglasses and saw her gaze dart toward him for an instant. She was still a little jumpy around him, as though she didn't quite trust him. He wanted to change that attitude. In a hurry.

She was a mass of contradictions, and that intrigued him. Wholesome, sexy, shy and sweet, with a hint of steel at her core. She had the glossy lips of a siren, the delicate face of an angel—and a tattoo.

Hell, he was getting hot. And not from the sun beating down on his head.

"So, what do you usually do on weekends? Besides bird-watching, that is." They were skirting downtown San Diego now. He automatically noted one of Carracell Inc.'s retail stores in a strip mall off to the right. The cell phone business was booming, and this particular location drew a lot of customers.

"Friday and Saturday nights, I work at Diamond Jim's. During the day, and on Sundays, I try to catch up on chores and studying."

"Hmm. So, you're going to school five days and working six nights—"

"Five. I'm off on Sunday and Monday."

"That's good to know."

She glanced over at him. He just smiled.

"Still, doesn't leave much time for a social life," he said.

"It hasn't been a difficult sacrifice. I made the decision when I enrolled at the university, and that's that."

"Are you saying you haven't had a boyfriend since you started school?" He saw her hands tighten on the steering wheel. That little gesture made him curious.

"I started school when I was five. Let's see, I went

steady with Terry Small in the third grade. And then there was a torrid fling with Chad Holkum at the end of fourth year..." She glanced at him. "Did you want the entire list?"

He liked her sass. Even though he detected that it hid deeper emotions. The very pleasantness of her tone told him he was trespassing where she didn't want him to go.

Since he'd never been one to pay much attention to warning signs, he winked at her. "We can save that for the next date. What I was fishing for, and doing a bad job of it at that, was more along the lines of recent men. Just wondering about my competition."

"Since there's not going to be a relationship between us, competition isn't relevant."

"Victoria," he said on a sigh, "you are a difficult woman. But never fear. I'm a patient man. And I love a challenge."

"I'm not challenging you, Jace." She pulled into the entrance of Torrey Pines State Reserve Park. Parking in the lot, she shut off the engine and turned to him. "I'm not interested."

"No?" He held her gaze, brushed a finger against a stray wisp of hair that clung to her cheek. Her eyes belied her words. Hooking his hand around the back of her neck, he drew her forward, slipped off her sunglasses. "Let's see."

He'd caught her off guard, but after only the slightest resistance, her lips went pliant beneath his. If she'd fought him, pulled back in earnest, he'd have immediately let her go. But just as her eyes had contradicted, so did her mouth. It was sweet, hungry…and definitely interested.

She tasted like his destiny.

The thought skittered through his head, should have surprised him, made him nervous. The only thing he could truly think about right now, though, was the intoxicating, electrifying tumult of desire that gripped his body like a vice and held him in thrall.

Despite her admitted lack of social life, Victoria Meadland knew how to kiss. She damned near melted his bones and fried his brain.

He wanted more, pulled her tighter against him, angled his head and feasted, surprised to find himself hard-pressed to keep up with her. He'd meant to prove a point to her. He was the one getting the lesson.

A car door slammed and the sound of a child's voice lifted in glee pierced his impassioned haze.

Jace lingered for another moment, then broke the kiss. Softly. Slowly.

He watched as her lids lifted to reveal dazed, beautiful blue eyes.

"Didn't feel uninterested to me."

Coherency flashed in her eyes with the speed of a powerful microprocessor. She scooted away from him, tucked her hair behind her ear, fumbled for the sunglasses he'd removed.

"Sexual chemistry doesn't make a relationship."

"No, but it helps." He noted that her hands were trembling.

"Jace, I told you, I'm not looking for anything more than friendship."

"But I am."

Her release of breath held more than frustration. "I think this was a bad idea. Maybe we should just call it a day." She reached for the ignition key.

He put his hand over hers, stilling her movements. He didn't know what made Victoria Meadland try to shy away from men—or from him—but he vowed to find out.

"We haven't even *begun* the day. I'd ask you if it was me, but after that kiss, it'd be a pretty stupid question."

She stared out at the tall pines that perfumed the air, then took off her sunglasses and turned to him. In her eyes were secrets and a vulnerability she desperately tried to mask. The combination made his heart sting, made him want to gather her close and promise her the world.

A world where everything was nice and tidy and pretty.

"I've made mistakes, Jace. I don't want to repeat them."

He put a finger over her lips. "I'm not interested in the past. We all have one, and all of us screw up at one time or another. But we all deserve a second chance as well. Can't you let yourself have that chance?"

She glanced away, pulling inward to a place he feared he couldn't reach. "I'm scared," she admitted softly.

"Hell, so am I. I don't usually come on so strong to a woman, but you touch something inside me."

"Jace—"

He stopped her again, this time reaching for her hand. "Let's put this on hold, okay? We got a little side-tracked and we're supposed to be bird-watching."

"You can't really want to go scouting for birds."

"I absolutely do. And just think. You can use me for a sounding board, educate me on our residential winged creatures. It'll be just like answering questions on a test. Difference is, I won't know if you're giving the correct answer or not, so either way, you ace the exam."

Her smile started slowly, then blossomed. "That's the most ridiculous attempt to get your way that I've ever heard. Sounds to me like you're not going to be of much help as a study aid."

He grinned, squeezed her hand again just to please himself. "Try me."

Chapter Three

She took him on the Guy Fleming Trail because it was an easy walk. Although he was in fabulous shape, and his tennis shoes were top quality and would manage most any terrain, she herself enjoyed this loop of the park. It was less traveled by tourists, who usually chose the beach trail.

"It's peaceful here," he said, looking up at the huge pines. "I've lived in San Diego all my life and never come here."

"You're probably into roller-blading or running along the boardwalks or parks by the beach, I bet."

He grinned. "How'd you guess?"

"It shows." She gave his body a quick scan to prove her point.

"You're good for my ego."

"As if it needs any help," she said dryly.

"Surely you're not accusing me of being conceited."

She thought about that for a moment. Actually, he wasn't stuck on himself. Just self-assured. "I was teasing—oh, look.'' She held out an arm, stopping him. Four quail chicks had ventured out for a drink in the birdbath just ahead of them.

"Little suckers, aren't they?" Jace said.

"Shh." Too late. The sound of his voice sent the mama quail out of the bushes where she'd been keeping watch. In seconds she had her babies rounded up and filed back into the cover of the bushes.

Vickie sighed. "There are rules to bird-watching. The first one is to be quiet."

He looked sheepish. "I knew that."

For the next few minutes, he walked beside her in silence, but she could feel the intangible vibration coming from him. He was dying to talk.

Unable to stand it any longer, she paused at the North Overlook and brushed her fingers against the prickly needles of a pine. "What?" she demanded.

His blond brows raised.

"You look like you're about to burst."

"I'm trying to be quiet." He reached down and scooped up a handful of pine needles. "I'm usually pretty good at following rules. This one's difficult."

"Why? Don't you enjoy the solitude of nature?"

"Sure. When I'm not with a beautiful woman."

The compliment shot straight to her head, chipped at her resolve to keep things light.

"We can talk. Most of the birds are in the trees and they'll pretty much ignore us." Like the scrub jay busily gathering seeds out of a pine cone a few yards away.

He let out a relieved sigh. "So, don't you need to be taking notes?"

"I've got a good memory. I'm more of a visual person, anyway. Most of the species, I've already looked up. I just like to come and see them in person rather than looking at a glossy picture. Besides, I love these old trees, the smell of them, what they represent."

"Trees are trees."

She smiled. "You've been living in the city jungle for too long. Your appreciation of the finer things in life appears to be lacking."

"I appreciate fine things. Except, maybe opera. I'm sorry to say, I just can't get into that. Or the ballet."

She started them walking along the trail again. "I've never personally experienced either one, but I've read about them and seen some on television. I think I'd enjoy the ballet more than the opera."

"Really?" He sounded appalled, yet resigned, as though he'd offer to take her if that's truly what she wanted.

She tugged his sleeve when he slowed down, and he slid his hand down to link with hers. For a second, she started to resist. They shouldn't be walking hand in hand like lovers. But the warmth of his big palm felt comforting. Solid. Like the pines that surrounded them.

The trees in this section of the reserve weren't the rarest or the tallest of the species, but the moment she'd stumbled upon them several years ago, she'd identified with them. Along the sea cliffs, their roots grew in poor soil, they suffered from drought, were blasted by storms and cooked in the sun, yet they survived.

Vickie, too, had endured her share of hard times, but she hadn't given up. She'd survived.

When she left her hand in his, he gave a squeeze as if to say thanks. Her heart throbbed in her chest and she suddenly couldn't think of a thing to say. Life didn't get much better than this.

Here she was walking through one of her favorite places. And here was this man with gilded hair and laughter in his eyes. A strong, capable man who excelled in the business world, yet remained so humanly, genuinely down to earth.

And he was with her.

"You've gone quiet," he commented. "Are you taking mental notes?"

"Yes." Just not on the birds. "It's easy to get caught up in the serenity."

"The beach is pretty serene."

"Yes, but that's the trail that most of the tourists take." They were at the South Overlook now and she nudged him over toward a pretty clearing by the cliffs.

"Man, look at that," he said. "You can see clear to Catalina Island."

"That impresses you? You've got an excellent view right off your own deck at your condo."

"Yeah, but the weather's not always cooperative, and the island stays hidden." He lifted their joined hands, pointed toward the south. "That's La Jolla. See that hill over there?"

She leaned in close, smelled the fresh air scent on his clothes, the subtle hint of spice on his skin. She nearly lost her concentration, then followed the direction of their joined hands. "The one with the mansions scattered on top?"

"Well, yeah. But I never considered them mansions. My parents live on that hill." He dropped their hands back to his side but didn't let go.

"You grew up there?"

"Mostly. They bought the house about twenty years ago."

"Must have seemed like paradise to you. Not that your condo isn't like a slice of Eden."

Jace glanced down at her, surprised by the whisper of envy, yet genuine appreciation. He'd taken his homes for granted, rarely saw them through anyone's eyes but his own familiar ones. He kept forgetting that Vickie had grown up in what she'd termed Hell's Home.

She was so beautiful. Not like a model or movie star all made-up for the public. She was fresh and wholesome. Her skin was smooth and sun-kissed with a sprinkle of pale freckles. Full lips, lake-blue eyes, a no-fuss hairstyle that left it silky and straight, long enough to brush her shoulders. The kind of hair that made a man want to run his hands through it, feel it tickling against his chest, his...

"Uh, why don't we sit for a minute."

"Sure."

He'd meant to take advantage of the bench, but Vickie moved close to the edge of the overlook, bent down to test the dampness of the ground and sat among the packed dirt and pine needles, drawing her knees up and wrapping her arms around them. He joined her on the ground, took a moment to listen to the sound of the sea and chatter of birds, missing the feel of her hand in his.

A gull winged overhead, squealing as he soared and kept an eye out for food treasures in the sea or tidbits left on the beach by careless walkers.

"Do seagulls count as bird-watching subjects?"

"Yes," she said with an indulgent smile.

"Well, then, we've got a front row seat to do some serious watching." He propped an arm on his bent knee and sifted his fingers through the pine needles strewn on the ground.

"I bet you've loved living on the ocean all your life." Her voice was soft and wistful as she gazed out at the sea.

"It's the best."

"Do you sail?" she asked.

"Mmm. I've got a little catamaran I take out several times a month. And a sixty-foot Michaelson that's a honey of a sports fisher. It's great for weekend trips to Catalina Island, too. Have you ever been over there?"

"No."

"I'll take you. It's also cool to cruise the harbor at night, watch the sunset and look at the lights. We should plan that, as well."

"Whoa. With all these plans, how do you get any work done?"

"I'm one of those nasty larks you mentioned this

morning. I get up early, take care of business when the phones aren't ringing like mad. Plus, I have an incredibly qualified staff to handle the day-to-day running of things. They're a great group of people, most of them have been with me from the start of the company. If I decided to retire tomorrow, the company would run without me.''

''Could you just let it go like that? I mean, it's your baby, so to speak. Wouldn't you miss it?''

''Maybe. I've taken it pretty well to the top, and we've been lucky enough to stay there. Sometimes I get an itch to try something different, though. Nothing like a new venture to stir the blood. As you probably know with your studies and plans for teaching.''

''My teaching's certainly not going to make me millions like your cell phone business obviously has done for you.''

''But you'll be following your bliss.''

She looked over at him, hugged her bent knees tighter. ''That's a neat way of putting it.''

''It's true. No matter what you choose to do in life, it should be something you love, something you're passionate about. I've heard that passion in your voice when you talk about teaching, seen your dedication to school and studying. I admire that. If I didn't think you were into it, I'd be trying to steer you in another direction.''

''A meddler, are you?''

He grinned. ''Probably. My sister says so. She's always buried in her science experiments and I'm hounding her to get out and interact with people more.

She's got great qualities but she isolates herself instead. I guess I can get carried away sometimes putting in my two cents worth, but I like to see the people around me, especially the people who matter to me, be the best they can be.''

Vickie rubbed her hands over the ribbed cotton sleeves of her sweater, watched the enthusiasm on his handsome face as he warmed to his subject. His optimism was contagious. And with regard to her, it was thrilling.

He believed she was the best she could be. The implied compliment touched her more deeply than a bucket of diamonds laid at her feet.

She'd been *taught* she wasn't good enough. A gesture here, a cutting word there. Growing up, it had been as though she were invisible, of no consequence to anyone. Just a body taking up space and an extra mouth to feed.

Jace touched her cheek, startled her. ''Where'd you go all of a sudden?''

She gazed out at the sea, to the hill scattered with luxury homes, one of them his family's. ''When I was fifteen, I skipped school with a friend. Her parents were at work, so we hung out at her house. We listened to music, mooned over boys, nipped into a bottle of wine and sampled a few other brands of liquor behind their wet bar. I found out pretty quick that mixing various types of alcohol has pretty awful consequences.'' She paused and watched as a flock of pelicans took flight from the marsh and landed at the ocean's edge to wade in the waves.

"Tracy's mom caught us and drove me back to the group home. I just wanted to curl up and die someplace. Although she scolded us for the drinking, she figured heaving up our toenails was punishment enough. She was gentle with me, amused in a way."

"I'm guessing the folks at Hell's Home weren't so amused?"

She smiled at the way he used her disrespectful name for Helen's Home. "No, Helen wasn't amused. She said she'd expected as much from me. That I'd come from trash and would be trash for the rest of my life."

Jace cursed and put his arm around her. "But you didn't believe her."

"Oh, yes I did. For a while at least." She liked the feel of his arm around her but didn't like the direction of the conversation. She didn't know why she'd told him that, could still feel the shame, the hurt, the isolation.

"So, anyway," she said, flicking her hair behind her ear, "I appreciate you saying what you did. About being the best I can."

He pressed his lips gently against her temple. She could have turned into him, would have welcomed the intimacy, but he simply rested his head against hers, sat quietly and watched the waves break in frothy curls, rushing onto shore and ebbing out again.

WHEN SHE PULLED into the driveway of Jace's condo later that day, she left the car running so she wouldn't be tempted to prolong the day. After only spending a short amount of time with him, she couldn't believe how well they hit it off. He was easy to be with, brought out the best in her.

Jace reached over and shut off the ignition key himself. ''How about some dinner before you head off for work?''

She shook her head. ''No time. I need to type up a quick paper on my notes about today, then be at the bar by six.''

''Notes? Will I be included in them?''

She couldn't resist his sexy smile. ''I don't think my science professor would go for that.''

''Hey, I contributed. I pointed out the seagull, didn't I?''

''And scared off the baby quail.''

''Sorry about that.'' He brushed his knuckles over her cheek. ''I don't want the day to end.''

''I have to work or I won't be able to indulge in your favorite subject. Eating. Honestly, I don't know how you stay in such great shape.''

''Mmm. More compliments on my physique. We're making progress.''

She laughed. ''Get out of my car, Jace Carradigne. You'll make me late.''

''Kiss me goodbye?''

She shook her head. ''I can't think when you kiss me.''

''I said *you* kiss *me*. I promise to let you do all the work.''

''You think that'll make a difference?''

"Won't know till we give it a try. In the interest of an experiment, I'm willing to sacrifice myself."

"Does anyone ever tell you no?"

"Sure. Lots of times."

His mouth was so close, smiling and inviting. The temptation was bigger than she was. "Okay. Keep your hands in your lap."

"Yes, ma'am."

Stifling a bubble of laughter, she leaned over and brushed her lips against his. The spark was just as strong as a full-out kiss. What the heck. In for a penny and all that.

She touched the side of his face, watched his eyes deepen to the color of rich moss. This time when she leaned into him, her mouth was firm, direct and mobile. The tickle of laughter turned into a silent moan of intense need.

Although his hands remained in his lap as promised, he kissed her back. And oh, he was good at it.

Lost in the feel of him, she forgot that she was the one supposed to be in control. She raised her other hand to his face, and put everything she had into the kiss, determined to leave him with an impression he wouldn't soon forget.

She was playing with fire, and it wasn't fair, but she couldn't seem to help herself.

Finding that her own bones had turned liquid, she eased up, nibbled, toyed, then slowly slid back to her own side of the car.

He sat totally silent for endless minutes. Then he raked a hand through his hair. "Wow."

She was having a little trouble with her own breathing, so she just smiled.

"After that, you've got to promise to have brunch with me tomorrow."

"Did it ever occur to you that I might have other plans?"

"Sure. But then you set me straight on several different occasions, remember?"

Her insistence over not having or wanting a social life. "It's not nice to gloat when you're right."

"I grovel as well as I gloat." He grinned, and the power of those dimples was like a thrilling sock to her solar plexus.

"Mmm-hmm."

"You'd be doing me a huge favor. It's Sunday brunch at my parents' house. Although they're great people, things like that can be tedious."

"Your parents' house! I'm not crashing a family breakfast uninvited. I haven't even met them."

"You won't be crashing, I just invited you, and you'll meet them tomorrow."

"You can't just invite a guest to come home with you."

"Why not?"

"It might be awkward."

"My mother would be insulted if she heard that. She prides herself on making company feel welcome. Come on, Vickie. I want to spend time with you. And I'd like you to meet my parents. Say yes."

Going home to meet his parents seemed to be rushing things, yet she couldn't believe how much she wanted to do that. To meet the people he'd talked about, see how he'd lived, grown up.

"I don't know how you keep getting me to change my mind, but, yes."

He lifted her hand to his lips, kissed her knuckles. Stunned by the gesture, she could barely think.

"I'll pick you up at ten in the morning, then."

She nodded, watched him unfold his long, lean body and get out of the car. "Be careful driving home."

She merely nodded again, started the engine and backed out of the driveway.

He'd kissed her hand. Now how was a woman supposed to concentrate on driving after that?

HE WAS on her doorstep promptly at ten the next morning. With her nerves in a mess, she paused with her hand on the door, wondered if she should invite him in, hoped he wasn't the sort to roam and snoop. Her bedroom looked like a teenager had gone in there and thrown a major tantrum.

Giving her appearance one last check in the hall mirror, she took a breath to calm her nerves. She hadn't known what to wear for a meet-the-parents brunch, and had tried on every one of her meager outfits, finally settling on a pair of black slacks, and a knit turtleneck sweater in soft heather. A black leather hip belt matched her chunky calf-high boots. The extra three-inch height the boot soles gave her made her feel a little more confident.

She opened the door, and her nerves skittered all

over again. Jace Carradigne was the epitome of the word male.

"Hi." He held out a slim velvet box. "This is for you."

"For what?" Sissy inched out from behind the couch, checking out the strange man in her domain.

"Just because."

Her heart pumped. Slowly, she lifted the hinged lid, then sucked in a breath. The bracelet was simple in design, made of delicate gold links with tiny heart-shaped charms set with brilliant sapphires."

"Oh, my gosh. It's beautiful. I don't know what to say. I can't...I shouldn't—"

"If you're going to tell me you shouldn't accept it, you'll hurt my feelings."

"But it's too much." She couldn't resist running her finger over the cool stones.

"I saw it when I was poking around some shops this morning and thought of you. It matches the rings you wear."

She automatically fingered the two sapphire rings on her finger. She'd bought them herself. Other than her watch and a couple of pairs of earrings, they were the only jewelry she owned.

Emotions worked in her throat. No one had ever bought her jewelry. And she'd received precious few gifts in her life. The homes she'd lived in growing up hadn't had funds or the inclination to spend foolishly on kids who were only temporary.

"You shouldn't be spending this kind of money on me."

"Vickie, I've made a fortune and I'm dying to spend it. You don't make it easy, so I decided to take matters into my own hands."

"Well." She admired the bracelet, wondered why she felt weepy all of a sudden. "You handle matters very well. Thank you."

"You're welcome." Since she still hadn't invited him in, he stepped over the threshold, took the box from her and lifted the bracelet out. "Here, let me put it on for you."

She held out her wrist. Chills raced up her arm as his fingers brushed against her skin. She stared at the top of his head as he bent over his task. Everything inside her wanted to fall. For him. It was an old pattern. An old habit.

But maybe this time would be different.

Take it slow, Vickie. Don't rush.

He looked up at her, smiled softly. "Ready to go?"

The sapphire hearts tinkled merrily as she lowered her hand. Oh, damn it. She was going to cry after all. Tears welled, even though she fought like mad to battle them back.

Rather than making her feel foolish, he simply swept a gentle thumb across her cheek, wiped away the moisture, then pulled her to him and placed a tender kiss on her forehead. "That's the best thank-you I've ever received over a gift," he whispered.

"I feel like an idiot."

This time he kissed her eyelids, her cheeks. "You're perfect."

If he'd pushed even the slightest, she would have

closed the door behind him and invited him into her bedroom, never mind the mess. But he didn't press, didn't take advantage, never even came close to her lips.

He was a man of honor, integrity, and the best kind of gentleman.

And despite her sternest warnings to herself, she was terribly afraid she was falling in love.

Chapter Four

Linking his hand with hers, Jace led her out the door to his car.

A sporty, obscenely expensive black Porsche.

"Looks to me like you're doing a good enough job spending," Vickie said as she slipped into the fragrant leather bucket seat.

He grinned. "I have a passion for speed."

"Tell me about it," she muttered to herself as he shut the passenger door and jogged around to the driver's side. She glanced down at the bracelet on her right wrist. The sun glanced off the brilliant stones, casting speckled prisms across the gray leather dash of the car.

Darn it, she was beginning to feel like a princess. And that wasn't an ideal she should let herself get used to.

"Buckle up," he said as he slid into the driver's seat and started the powerful engine.

She obeyed, glanced at him. "Do you plan to speed?"

"I'll try to keep the shiny side of the car up."

"I feel so much more comfortable now."

He laughed. "Relax and enjoy."

"Tough to relax when I'm crashing Sunday brunch at your parents' house."

"You're not crashing. I called ahead, and Mom's tickled to death." He whipped the car into a tight turn and zipped onto the bridge. "Those were her exact words."

"I've never been home to meet a guy's parents before."

"You're kidding. Didn't any of your boyfriends have families?"

She shrugged. "Guess not."

He reached over and linked his hand with hers, pulling it over to rest on the gear shift. "Good. Not that the poor saps didn't have families," he said. "I like it that I'm your first."

For a moment, she thought he was referring to her virginity—which was definitely lacking. Then she realized he was speaking of taking her home to interact with his family. Nerves skittered once more.

"Tell me about your parents."

"Dad's a doctor—a gynecologist actually. He delivers babies. You never know when he'll have to excuse himself from dinner or a party and race off to the hospital."

"Bet that makes it tough for your mom to nail down plans."

"She's totally cool about it. He loves what he does, and that makes her happy."

"And your mom? What does she do?"

He glanced over at her, grinned. "She's a college professor...of psychology."

Vickie's eyes widened. Surely she wasn't enrolled in a psychology class taught by Jace's mother. No, her professor's name was Spinneley. "At San Diego State?"

"No. At U.C.S.D. in La Jolla."

"Oh."

"Still, the two of you will have plenty to talk about. Teaching for one. And if you've got questions about your class or assignments, she'd be glad to launch into a lengthy dissertation."

"Ah, one of those who likes to give the whole of the answer rather than the shortcut."

"Exactly. I hated to ask her for help with homework when I was a kid. She loves knowledge and information and solving puzzles. And she believes in being thorough. I'd want a quick answer, and she'd spend an hour tutoring."

"Cut into your time playing video games, hmm?"

"Video games and basketball. The guys would come by for me and end up getting classroom instruction before we could go out and practice."

"Did they mind?"

"Naw. Half my pals were pretty stoked on my mom. Weird when your friends are ogling your mom's butt in a pair of tight jeans. She's beautiful, as you'll see. She's fifty-five and still has a body that won't quit. Even cooler, after she'd make us all study, she'd go out in the driveway and shoot baskets with us."

"She sounds wonderful," Vickie said wistfully.

"She is. She's really grounded. Ambitious, but superdedicated to her family."

What would it have been like to grow up with a mother like that? Heaven, she thought.

"What are their names?"

"Annie and Chris. Christopher—my dad."

"I figured that one out on my own," she said dryly, feeling her insides tumble in nervous anticipation.

Glancing out the window, she drank in the scenery as they began a steep climb along a sea cliff road with hairpin turns and incredible views.

They'd traveled about twelve miles from downtown San Diego into the seaside suburb of La Jolla. Mediterranean style architecture comprised of arches, colonnades, red-tile roofs and pale stucco dotted the landscape.

Set high on a hill overlooking the coastline and a pretty cove with a private sandy beach, Jace parked the Porsche in an enormous driveway of what Vickie could only consider a true mansion.

Even in fall, colorful flowers drenched planters and walkways with vivid color. Expansive lawns were linked by stone paths, aged trees and unique fountains where birds bathed happily in the splashing water. Above one of the garage doors, looking slightly out of place amid so much grandeur was a well-used basketball hoop—no doubt the one Jace and his friends had practiced on after school.

Despite its size and obvious opulence, the house had a welcoming feel to it.

Before he'd even shut off the Porsche's engine, the front door of the house opened and his mother and father came out to greet them.

Annie was every bit as beautiful as Jace had said. She barely looked forty, even though Vickie knew she was fifteen years past that milestone mark. Short, dark hair framed a face that would definitely turn men's heads.

And his father—light blond hair, at least six foot, trim…he reminded her of the actor Robert Redford. She imagined his patients fell in love with him on a daily basis.

"I see where you get your great genes," she commented, when Jace opened her car door to help her out.

"You speaking about my pants or my bod?" he asked, raising his eyebrows suggestively.

"Your face, actually. But don't let it swell your head."

His smile was as bright as the sun pouring over them. He slipped an arm around her shoulders. "Come on. I'll introduce you."

His parents met them halfway. He hugged his mother, then his father. "Mom, Dad, I'd like you to meet Vickie Meadland." He winked. "Treat her nice. She's special."

Vickie's face flamed. She wished he wouldn't say things like that. But oh, it felt wonderful.

"It's nice to meet you both."

Annie cupped one of Vickie's hands between both of hers, gave a squeeze. "We're tickled you could join us. We're Annie and Chris. We don't go in for a bunch of formality stuff. Okay with you?''

''Um, fine.'' She noted that Jace winked at her when his mother repeated that she was ''tickled.'' Just as he'd said.

Chris shook Vickie's hand. ''Come on in. Annie's been cooking up a storm.''

''Oh, I have not. I made an oven French toast that's easy as pie, and an egg casserole.''

A place this size and she did her own cooking? Vickie thought. She'd imagined servants scurrying about discreetly.

''Uh-oh,'' Jace said. ''You must want something from me if you're fixing my favorite French toast.''

Annie gave his arm a fond whack. ''You're an insolent child. And I cooked it with Vickie in mind, not you. Kelly!'' she hollered as they passed the wide, curving stair case, causing Vickie to jump. ''Breakfast!''

Neither Jace nor Chris appeared surprised at the forceful bellow that had come out of this elegant woman.

''Ha,'' Jace said, looping his arm around Vickie's shoulders. ''I think my feelings are hurt.''

''You'll live,'' Annie said, laughing happily. Chris merely walked quietly beside his wife, gazing at her with amused indulgence and a love so bright it made the heart squeeze.

''Your mother insisted on eating on the patio,'' Chris said. ''I've got the heaters lit. The sun's nice, but there's a nip in the breeze.''

The patio covered a good quarter of an acre, broken up by a crystal blue swimming pool and splashing waterfall. Gulls wheeled overhead, diving beyond the cliff. The sound of the ocean's surf vied with the water rushing over rocks, spilling into the mosaic tile-rimmed pool.

Jace pulled out a chair for her, and she sat, just as another woman came rushing out the door.

"Ah, the absentminded professor's decided to join us," Jace teased. "I'm surprised you're not bedding down on a cot in that lab you love so much."

Kelly shrugged. "Mom said I had to be home for brunch."

"Twenty-six and still doing what mom says?"

"Absolutely," Annie answered for her daughter. "And I taught you better manners. Introduce Vickie to your sister."

"Yes, ma'am. Vickie, this is my sister, Kelly. The one I told you about who likes to blow up things."

"I don't blow up things," Kelly said, shyly meeting Vickie's eyes. "Nice to meet you."

She was quiet, thin and a bit gangly. Her long, tightly curled blond hair was scraped back in a messy ponytail as though she couldn't be bothered with it. Studious glasses framed light green eyes that appeared distracted, as though she'd been in deep thought and had been disturbed, hadn't quite shaken free of the trance.

Absentminded professor seemed fairly accurate. Yet Vickie could see that the excellent family genes had filtered down to Kelly Carradigne as well. She just didn't accent those genes, chose instead to live inside her brilliant mind.

"Jace told me you've been working on a cure for unique viruses," she said.

Kelly's eyes flashed with excitement in the space of a heartbeat. Ah, here indeed, was her passion. "Yes. Right now I'm working on developing antigens for A.C.I.—Atypical Coronary Infusion. It's a fatal virus that affects the blood flow to the heart. It's most prevalent in older men, and we've determined that it isn't hereditary. I've been lucky that I've gotten some excellent grants to fund my research, and I'm on the verge of a breakthrough. The lab mice are responding beautifully. I'm ready to go for clinical trials…"

Her words trailed off and she shrugged sheepishly. "Sorry. I get carried away."

"It sounds fascinating," Vickie said. "And what you're doing for mankind is invaluable."

The compliment obviously pleased Kelly, yet she seemed to withdraw into her own private world once more, as though she'd forgotten that the family was gathered around the table, enjoying fabulously fluffy French toast caramelized with brown sugar and pure maple syrup.

As they ate, Jace and his father caught up on each other's lives and businesses, and Vickie was content to let the conversation flow around her, soaking it all up, learning small details here and there about all of their personalities.

This is what she'd always craved, she realized. A family who joked and talked and loved unconditionally. She'd spent so many years running from herself and her sins. Yet all she'd ever really wanted—at least the *core* of that want—was a home and family. To belong.

She had to be careful. It would be easy to imagine herself belonging to this happy group of people. Especially now that her emotions toward Jace had taken such a strong hold on her heart.

But planning the wedding and the kids to come was foolish. She hadn't been totally honest with him. Oh, she'd never lied, but there were things he should know about her. Things that might change his opinion of her.

She could well be setting herself up for an incredible fall.

FROM ACROSS the room, Jace watched as Vickie stacked dishes in the kitchen and laughed at something his mom said. He'd known the two of them would find plenty in common, with his mom being a teacher and Vickie so determined to pursue a similar career.

It pleased him that she got along so well with his family. That was important to him.

Because family was important to him.

His dad came up beside him, rested a hand on his shoulder.

"She's quite a gal," Chris said.

"Yes. I think she's the one."

Chris's palm tightened in a squeeze of acknowledgment and acceptance. "I should lecture you on making quick decisions, but I knew within minutes that your mother was the one for me. Is Victoria of the same mind as you?''

"Don't know. I haven't told her yet.''

"Word of advice, son. You don't *tell* a woman anything. You ask. Nicely.''

Jace grinned. "Thanks for the tip.''

"Well, you don't need too many tips from me, but I know you. You're like a strong wind, sweeping everyone along in your wake. Most of us are happy that we've traveled the distance with you, but women can get a little touchy when they think they've been manipulated.''

"I thought that was a guy thing—resisting manipulation.''

Chris shook his head. "We men are the least complicated of the species—don't tell your mother I said that.''

"My lips are sealed.'' He took his hands out of his pockets. "Thanks for making Vickie feel welcome. I think I'll go convince her to spend some one-on-one time with me.''

"She's an easy lady to welcome. Good luck, son.''

TUESDAY NIGHT, when she went back to work at the bar, Vickie was experiencing a sort of Jace withdrawal syndrome. This was the first full day since they'd begun dating that she hadn't seen him.

Dating, she thought. She'd tried to tell herself that they were only friends. Yet it sure felt like dating.

Sunday after brunch at his parents, he'd taken her for a walk along the Mission Bay boardwalk, bought them each a kite and competed with her shamelessly, then cajoled her into riding the beautifully restored classic wooden roller coaster.

Afterward he'd prepared a late supper at his condo, kissed her beneath the moonlight on the beach below his balcony and driven her home. Monday after school, he'd showed up at her door and whisked her off to an elegant dinner at a wonderful Mediterranean bistro where the menus didn't even list the prices.

He hadn't pressed her for anything more than her time and a few kisses. Potent, mind-blowing kisses.

She was beginning to feel as though she was living the best part of Cinderella's life.

"Oh, my gosh. What is this?" Tiffany exclaimed, grabbing Vickie's wrist to inspect the bracelet that tinkled every time she moved.

Vickie set her tray of empties on the bar before she dropped the whole thing and had a mess of glass to clean up.

"A gift."

"From the cell phone guy?"

"His name is Jace. And, yes, if you must know, he gave it to me."

"Is it your birthday? God, I'd feel like a heel if I missed—"

"No, it's not my birthday."

Tiffany's kohl-rimmed eyes widened, danced with an I-told-you-so expression. Obviously not content to let her features speak for her, she said, "See there. The man's a goner."

"He just has more money than he knows what to do with and likes to spend. It's no big deal."

"Honey, eighteen-karat gold and honest to God gems are a big deal. Did you sleep with him?"

"Tiffany!" She glanced around to see if anyone in the busy club was paying attention. Paul was polishing glasses behind the bar. His raised brows either indicated that he'd heard, or were a warning that they should get back to work.

"Well, *I'd* sleep with him. The guy's a hunk. There's something dynamic about him with an added…I don't know, a kind of best friend, boy-next-door quality. That's a lethal combination."

"Tell me about it," Vickie said before she could censure herself. "But we haven't…you know. I'm not jumping into a relationship. I don't have room in my life for one."

"That's bull. And you don't have to have a relationship to have sex."

"Been there, done that," Vickie reminded her friend. "And I'm trying like mad not to repeat past mistakes."

"You can't base everything in your future on your past, hon. You've grown, learned. Besides, Jace is different than that sleazebag who's doing time in the pen. Or the boy you ran off with. You can't even begin to compare them."

Being reminded of her past brought the familiar punch of shame. She knew she'd made huge strides in her life in the past ten years, but the fact that she'd *allowed* herself to base her happiness and existence on the wrong men still had the power to sting.

"What's with you singing Jace Carradigne's praises all of a sudden? Did he put you up to giving him references?"

Tiffany laughed and passed her drink order ticket to Paul. "No, but since the boss man's obviously taken, I'd like to have a shot at one of his pals—and I figure you could set me up. I mean, you don't find too many successful, well-adjusted guys who are willing to blatantly play matchmaker."

"First off, the boss man's not taken. And his friends weren't playing matchmaker. They were just joking around, telling me little tidbits about Jace because he'd put them up to it so he could get a date."

"Did they tell you anything that wasn't true?"

Vickie thought about that. Chad had talked about Jace's honesty, honor and integrity. Frank had expounded on his buddy's optimistic, positive attitude, his boundless energy, and sense of humor—and his wealth, of course.

All of that was dead-on.

"I have to get back to work," she said evasively. She scooted behind the bar to clear her tray and load it up again with the drinks Paul had mixed.

"You do that," Tiffany said with a bright smile. "I'll just go seat your man in your section so you'll have a good excuse to spend a little time talking to a customer."

Vickie's pulse leapt and pounded in her veins. Sure enough, Jace had come in the door. Their eyes met across the room and the floor seemed to shift beneath her feet. Either that or her knees were melting.

Everything within her shifted, jumbled together in a mass of emotions, then settled in a warmth that bathed from the inside out.

To have a man be so attentive was the ultimate fantasy. She didn't wonder if he would call, didn't worry that his eyes were roving, looking for a better deal.

He made her feel as though she were the only one in the world for him.

And that both thrilled her and scared her to death.

MANHATTAN WAS beginning to bore him, and time wasn't moving fast enough to suit him.

The churning in his gut boiled like a cauldron of acid. Only the smooth nectar of his favorite scotch could cool the fire.

He hated waiting for phone calls. Waiting, waiting, waiting. He wanted action.

He gulped amber liquid, tipped more into the glass, splashing it over his hand. The sloppy miscalculation annoyed him. It was *their* fault. He shouldn't have to be relegated to behind-the-scenes, waiting in his apartment like some kind of prisoner.

He *deserved* to be at the top.

He *would* be. They owed it to him. All of them.

When the phone rang at last, a fine haze of red was blurring his vision. He thumbed the button of the phone that rarely left his hand, and raised it to his ear.

"Speak."

"We might have found something. There's a

woman. It looks serious. He took her to meet his parents.''

The haze before his eyes began to clear. ''Well, well. That could be a nice development.'' Although adding more players to the mix could get a little muddy. Too many accidents close together might raise suspicion.

However, no one was going to stand in his way.

He had a shrewd mind, the mind of a ruler. Yes, indeed.

''Get on it. I want everything you can find on her. Right down to her brand of toothpaste.''

He disconnected the phone, drained his glass and splashed another three fingers of the smooth amber liquid over ice.

Maybe he'd take another little trip. Outside his apartment window were gray skies and rain. Sunny California would be a nice change of pace.

Some female company would make it even better.

He giggled and lifted the phone to his ear again.

Sometimes you had to squash a bunch of unsuspecting whelps to get to the big dog.

Chapter Five

Vickie charged in the door and dumped her books on the kitchen table, grabbing the telephone on the fourth ring.

"Hello?"

"Hey, Vic, it's Paul from Diamond Jim's."

She rolled her eyes and hooked the phone between her shoulder and ear so she could deal with Sissy's water dish. The silly cat had dragged a dishrag and plopped it in the center of the bowl, soaking up all the moisture.

"I think I can recognize your voice after working with you for three years, Paul."

"Habit. Listen, babe, I'm calling to be your fairy godfather."

She laughed. "And how's that?"

"What would you say to the night off with full pay?"

"I'd say you've been smoking funny cigarettes. What's up?"

"Actually, my niece is in town. She's after getting

a little experience as a cocktail waitress, and I figured a hopping Friday night crowd would either make her a pro or change her mind and send her back to school.''

It still didn't add up. "So, why give me the night off?"

"Because I'm a nice guy?"

"Yeah, you're a nice guy, but I don't buy it."

"Look. Do you want the time off, or not?"

A free night—and pay to boot—was hard to turn down. Although she would miss out on her tips. And Friday night's were substantial. Still…

"Take advantage of my generosity and spend the extra time with your man," Paul suggested.

That's when it clicked. "Did Jace put you up to this?"

"Geez, you're so suspicious."

"Paul."

"What if he did?"

"Then I might be a tad annoyed."

"Hey, don't take it out on me. It's no skin off my nose if you work or not. But the part about my niece is on the level. She thinks she should hang out a while before she considers college. If we're a little under-staffed, I've got a better shot at making her cocktail-serving experience less than appealing."

Vickie relaxed. "That's very sneaky of you, Paul."

"Yeah, but I'm a great uncle otherwise."

"I'm sure you are. Okay, run the poor girl ragged. You want me back tomorrow?"

"Sure. If I can't make her cry 'uncle' in one night, it ain't gonna happen."

"Don't be too hard on her."

She hung up the phone and opened a can of tuna for Sissy. She needed to find time to get to the market. The cupboards were starting to look a bit skimpy.

Five minutes later, the phone rang again.

"One guess who that'll be," she said to the cat. "I ought to let the machine pick it up." But when it came to Jace Carradigne, she was a pushover.

Surprised that her heart was pounding since she'd been expecting the call, she took a breath, and lifted the receiver.

"Hi," Jace said softly. "How was your day?"

Darn it. The mere sound of his voice could make her melt like hot fudge in a microwave. "Decent...until I came home and got a strange phone call from work."

He paused, obviously picking up the pique in her voice. "And that phone call made your day, um, less decent?"

"Let's just say that I'm not real keen on someone organizing my life."

"Oh, man. I should have listened to my dad."

"Your dad's in on this, too?" Good grief. She was so mixed up she had to sit down. Sissy glanced up from her bowl of dinner, then went back to eating.

"No. He just advised me to *ask* first instead of planning when it comes to women."

"Women," she repeated, a prickle of annoyance rising at being lumped into a stereotypical group.

"Woman," he corrected quickly. "You're the only one in my life."

"Jace—"

"Come on, Vickie. I'm a poor student, but I promise to do better. You can even tell on me, if you like. Dad loves to gloat."

Idiot, she thought, hiding a smile. He could charm the habit off a nun if he set his mind to it. "How did you manage to get the club to pay my wages?"

"Hey, a guy's gotta have a few secrets."

She had a sneaking suspicion the money was coming out of his pocket rather than Diamond Jim's till.

"So, why did you arrange for me to have the night off?"

"Because I miss you. And I wanted to spend time with you without having to watch the clock. I'm headed out the door now to pick you up. Dress casual and warm. We're taking the boat out."

She sighed. "You really are a poor student. Forgot the lesson already."

He seemed at a loss. Then he laughed. "Sorry. Will you come out with me on my boat, Victoria? Let me ply you with dinner and wine? Relax with me under the stars?"

Oh, he knew how to paint a sensual picture. She ought to tell him no so he wouldn't think he could just toss his money and charm around like this.

But she wasn't about to penalize herself in the bargain. The man was flat-out irresistible. "On one condition."

"Name it."

"You promise not to go around organizing my life without permission."

"I love a woman who knows how to take charge and issue orders. See you in about twenty minutes."

The phone line disconnected. Vickie stared at it, then down at her cat, who was displaying good manners by cleaning her paws after her meal.

"Well. He's slick, I'll give him that. He slipped right around that condition and never gave a promise."

THE MARINA reminded Vickie of a crowded parking lot during a post-holiday sale. Instead of cars, though, there were boats. Tons of them.

Jace led her down a wooden plankway where enormous yachts shared the same prestigious address as smaller pleasure boats. Salt, sea and the faint smell of fish wafted on the late October breeze. The temperature had hovered in the eighties today. A typical, unpredictable day in California paradise.

Vickie shaded her eyes with her hand against the blinding glow of the setting sun. The constant screech of gulls and honking geese wintering over in the mild climate was like background music tuned at a higher than pleasant decibel.

She spotted the lettering on the boat before they actually reached it. *Carracell Inc.*

Good grief. He'd described it as a sports fishing boat. The thing was practically a ship. He must be one heck of a crackerjack driver to back this moving house into its slip without causing major damage. Only inches separated the dock from the boat's hull.

"Welcome aboard," Jace said, stepping lightly onto the rear deck of the boat and holding out a hand to assist her.

"I can't believe you called this a fishing boat."

"That's what it is. See the outriggers there?"

She had no idea what an outrigger was and rather than trying to take in too much at once, she focused on the grandeur around her.

"This is amazing," she murmured, moving forward without waiting for him to offer a tour. She was gawking, but there was no help for it. "I've never seen anything like it before." Perhaps that made her sound gauche, but she didn't care. Awe propelled her, leaving Jace to follow in her wake.

It was like looking at a piece of real estate at an open house. A very expensive piece of real estate.

Rich carpet in a velvet soft silver-gray, elegant wood trim, a bedroom bigger than the one in her apartment that looked as though it had been decorated by a professional interior designer, an efficient kitchen with all the latest gadgets and a sitting room furnished like something out of a design catalogue for the rich and famous.

She didn't imagine those were the correct terms to call the areas—this lifestyle was totally out of her realm of experience.

Jace had remained quiet as she touched and stroked the fabrics and textures around her. Once back in the enclosed living room, she turned to him.

"How in the world can you justify hauling smelly fish onto this swanky thing?"

He grinned. "We fishermen like our comfort. So you approve?"

She averted her eyes, pretended to consider. "It'll do."

Laughing, he placed a smacking kiss at the corner of her mouth. "I'm crazy about you."

She barely had time to register the kiss, or the zing of emotions before he was gearing up for action like a kid who couldn't wait to open gifts at his birthday party.

"Come on up to the bridge and we'll get this lady going."

Access to the second level of the boat was via a sturdy ladder. She climbed up behind him, glad she'd worn her jeans and tennis shoes.

Excitement winged through her. Never in her wildest dreams had she imagined herself experiencing this type of date.

"The skipper's domain," Jace announced, making a grand sweeping gesture with his hand.

It was just as fancy as the rest of the boat, with huge captain's chairs and enough gadgets to give a seven-forty-seven jet a run for its money. And the view...from this vantage point, it was incredible, like being on top of the world.

Jace started the engines, then headed back to the ladder. "I'll untie us. Be right back."

Vickie quickly studied her surroundings, afraid to touch anything. A compact refrigerator, efficient dining table and U-shaped seating area lined the walls.

The engines hummed, vibrating the floor beneath

her feet. Hopefully they wouldn't start floating off before he could get back up here and take the wheel. She didn't think she could steer this monster on a bet.

From the glass enclosure, she saw him releasing thick ropes, his muscles straining, his blond hair feathering in the wind. He was a pleasure to watch—a virile man who knew exactly what he was doing, seemed to handle any situation that came his way, laughed and smiled and simply enjoyed life. He didn't waste a single movement, was filled with energy and swept through his day like an offshore breeze racing a stopwatch and laughing at the sheer fun of it all.

With him, she felt safe.

A lot of people might take that for granted. But for Vickie, there had never been a time in her life she could remember that she'd truly felt safe. She'd only had herself to rely on. So it was a very big deal.

"All set," he said, his smile beaming as he leapt up the last rung of the ladder and slid into the thick leather seat. The pitch of the motors changed as he inched the boat out of the slip.

She couldn't help but admire his skill. The center waterway of the marina didn't look all that wide to her. And maneuvering a sixty-foot vessel was a little trickier than zipping a sports car out of a parking space.

"So, how many times did your insurance carrier drop you before you learned to do that?" she asked, somewhat surprised that he'd managed a slick pivot and they were now heading forward with plenty of room on either side of the boat.

Jace laughed. "I'll have you know, I've never had to file a claim. I'm good. I'll teach you, and we can work as a team."

A team. That sounded so perfect. "Do you like this boat?"

"I love it."

"Then you'll want to rethink asking me to drive it. I have enough trouble getting my car out of a parallel parking spot."

"I have faith in you. Just takes a little practice."

It seemed that every word he uttered, she wanted to put deeper connotations on, bask in them, her mind taking off in flights of fancy. She had to rein herself in, not make such a big deal out of casual statements. Even though she'd been starved all her life for exactly those type of statements.

They motored out of the marina, the engines kicking up a small wake and emitting diesel fumes from the slow pace.

"Look over there," he said pointing to the outcropping of rocks as they headed toward the breakwater.

She leaned forward, delighted at the sight of seals perched among the rocks, no doubt waiting for returning fishermen to toss them a snack. Not to be left out, gulls swooped and circled, as though afraid they'd miss a meal.

Laughter worked its way up her throat at the sheer joy of the evening. She waved at a group of people in a pleasure boat returning to the marina, and craned her neck to get a better look at two pelicans sitting on a steel buoy.

Jace glanced at her in gentle amusement, but she ignored him. She was going to soak up every drop of this experience, bask in it, store it in her memory.

The air was turning cool, but the enclosed bridge was cozy. The light bob of sea swelling against the hull soothed, draining away the stress of a hectic day at school. She allowed the luxurious leather seat to swallow her, cradle her.

"I'm surprised you don't live on this boat. Talk about instant destressing."

"I'm glad you like it."

They were out in the open sea now, cruising parallel with the shoreline. The boat's powerful engines left a V-shape trail of frothy white foam that matched the puffy clouds in the pale blue sky. At least a dozen seagulls played in the spray just off the boat's stern, wings arched, feet stretching as they dipped and swooped and kept a sharp eye out for food churned up in the wake.

Conversation didn't seem necessary, and the silence was a comfortable one. It was almost as though they'd been a couple for years, at ease with each other's company, secure enough that they didn't have to fill every moment with chatter.

Time seemed to stand still as the smell of sea air, diesel and perfection surrounded her. She could stay right here forever, she thought. It was as though the sea called to her, telling her she was home at last.

She heard the engines slow, listened to the lap of water against the hull, let the dreamy cadence and peacefulness engulf her.

"The sun's setting," Jace said, looking over at her.

She gazed toward the west where the sun was like a great orange ball, its bottom half already swimming below the horizon. The few clouds hanging low over the Catalina mountains took on glorious hues of color, from the palest pink of an abalone shell, to the fiery glow of a blazing Yule log.

"Isn't it amazing?" she whispered.

"Mmm. And it's also customary to kiss at sunset."

She whipped around to look at him. Eyes the color of clear emeralds were filled with a sensuality that both caressed and aroused. She felt her breath catch in her throat. "I've never heard of that custom."

He leaned over, tipped her face up toward his. "It's a Carradigne custom," he said, bringing his lips a mere breath away from touching. "A very old, very sacred custom."

Slowly, tenderly, he lowered his mouth to hers. The thrill that shot through her was powerful and drugging. Her hands crept up his shirtfront, to the nape of his neck. He pulled her right out of her seat, held her as close as two bodies could get, chests pressing, mouths savoring. She wrapped her arms around his neck, held on, never wanted him to let her go.

When his tongue lightly touched the seam of her lips, she opened, breathed in the sea air scent of him, reveled in the solid, safe-harbor feel of him. It was like floating on an exquisite dream, every nerve in her system dancing to the rapid beat of her heart.

Wanting him. Loving him.

He eased back, still holding her close. Her eyes

opened. "Shouldn't you be watching the road or something?"

His brows lifted, and he smiled, kissed her again.

"The water, I mean," she said against his mouth.

"I don't see any traffic, do you?"

All she saw was the two of them. In a private paradise. "I wouldn't want you to run us aground or anything."

"Trust me," he whispered.

She sighed, rested her forehead against his. "I do. And oddly enough, that scares me."

"Carradigne rule number two. No one's allowed to get scared unless it's Halloween. And that's three days off."

She shifted back into her seat, smiled at him. "The Carradignes seem to have a lot of rules and customs. Are you sure you're not just making them up as you go?"

He pressed a hand to his heart, tried to look affronted. And failed.

"Were you the type of kid who went around scaring people on Halloween?"

"Kid? I still do it. I've got a great Dracula costume. Fangs dripping blood, platform shoes that give me extra height, really creepy lenses that make my eyeballs glow."

"I hope it's for parties and you don't scare the poor little trick-or-treat children."

"Hey, somebody's got to pass out the candy. And the kids love it. Besides, there's another Carradigne rule…"

She laughed, delighted. "I might have known. What's this one?"

"I think it's number twenty-eight. No crying on holidays. Every trick-or-treater leaves my house smiling."

She shook her head. "You are a crazy man."

"And I'm a hungry man. What do you say we go below and have some dinner before the sunset completely fades away."

"If we go below, who's going to drive the boat?"

"I dropped the anchor."

She glanced out the window. Sure enough, they weren't moving. Lights rimmed the boat like a fancy house decked out for Christmas. The sea was calm, reflecting the colors of the sunset.

She followed him down the ladder, jolting when his hand wrapped around her thigh, then her waist to steady her. It nearly made her miss a step.

"Careful."

She nodded. If he'd kept his hands to himself she'd have been just fine.

She nearly did fall when she felt his hand slide into the waistband of her jeans, the backs of his fingers brushing her skin as he inched her sweater up higher.

"Sexy," he murmured, tracing the tattoo. "And sweet. I recognize the sunflowers and daisies. What's the other flower?"

She was looking at him over her shoulder, her knuckles no doubt white where they gripped the ladder, erotic chills chasing up and down her spine.

"Hydrangea," she said when her tongue unstuck itself from the roof of her mouth.

He grinned. "Most people go for a rose."

"Guess I'm not most people."

"Mmm. I like that. You bent over one night at the bar and your sweater rode up." He traced the tiny bouquet with the tip of his finger. "It was like seeing a little burst of exotic springtime. Drove me crazy."

His touch was driving *her* crazy.

He released her, helped her down the rest of the ladder. Good thing. She needed a minute to get her sea legs. The man could make her ache with arousal with a mere look.

In the galley, he took a bottle of white wine out of the refrigerator and poured them each a glass. Holding his aloft, he said, "To us."

Something in his eyes made her heart leap in her throat. It was as though he was saying so much more than just the two simple words.

She touched her glass to his, sipped, noted that he was watching her over the rim of his own drink.

Anticipation, sudden and keen, filled the air around them, pumped in her veins. A want like she'd never experienced gripped her, held her spellbound for endless moments.

He reached out, tenderly brushed his knuckles against her cheek. "Why don't you go enjoy the sunset while I put together something to eat?"

She shook her head. Surely she wasn't the only one who'd experienced that electrifying jolt. Two more seconds and she'd have dragged him down to the floor. "I'll help you. That way we can both enjoy it."

He set aside his glass, opened the fridge again. "Actually, there's not much to do. I confess, I cheated this time and had a catering company stock the galley."

"You just gave them the keys and let them stroll on in?" He took out several plates of salads, cold cuts, fruit bowls and bread.

"They didn't need a key. And besides, the company's bonded."

"I can't imagine not locking my possessions up tight." She took the stoneware dishes he set out and arranged them on the table. "Then again, some of the neighborhoods I've lived in haven't been the best."

"Those days are past, though," he said, placing the food on the table and holding out a chair for her to sit. "From this minute on, there's only the future."

She gazed at him. "You're always so positive, so sure."

"Yes."

"Are you ever…wrong? Or disappointed?"

"Not usually. When I know what I want, I'll use every resource available to get it." His eyes locked steadily onto hers. "When it's important, failure's not in my vocabulary."

Chills raced up her arms, and not from the sea air. Jace was the kind of man women dreamed about, the kind of man, she suspected, who gave his heart only once. And gave it all.

Perhaps it was the trick of the lights shining off the back of the boat, or perhaps it was her own foolish yearning, but for an instant, she believed he was giving his heart to her.

Oh, God. It would be a dream come true. Her life had been so rocky up to this point. But Jace had a way of making her feel like a princess. She wanted to clutch that feeling to her breast, hold it…live it, believe it.

For once, for as long as it lasted, she wanted to wear the glass slipper.

VICKIE LEANED against the railing of the boat, gazing at the lights of the homes on shore, watching as the headlights of the cars cruising down the coast highway winked in the dark. Jace came up behind her, rubbed her arms where the chill air seeped through her sweater.

"Want to know what Carradigne rule number four is?"

She smiled, leaned back against the warmth of his body. "I'm sure you're going to tell me."

"It's always kiss your lady after a dinner under the stars."

She turned in his arms, her back against the rail, his body against her front, and lifted her lips.

"Let's don't break any rules," she said.

"Mmm. My kind of woman." Jace gazed down at her for endless moments before he lowered his head. He intended the kiss to be light, but the moment he felt the warmth, the softness of her mouth, he was lost.

He wrapped his arms around her, nearly lifted her off the ground, held her as close as he could without crushing her. The urge to be inside her was nearly eating him alive.

Her lips were avid and aggressive, stunning him for a moment. Then he groaned, kissed her deeper, held her closer. Inching his hand beneath her sweater, he stroked the length of her spine, the sides of her rib cage, finally cupping her breast.

She sucked in a breath, and he paused. ''Too fast?''

''No,'' she whispered. ''Not fast enough.''

Those three words were worth more to him than a million dollar account. He rested his head against hers, trying to get his breath, his bearings, to remain in control.

''I didn't plan this, you know.'' He didn't want her to think he'd expected their evening to end up in bed. He'd hoped. Hell, he was a man. But he hadn't expected.

''I know.'' Her hands were cold as they framed his face, her eyes fiery hot. ''Make love with me, Jace.''

Chapter Six

He lifted her in his arms and headed toward the bedroom.

She nearly strangled him, clutching at his neck as though she feared he'd drop her. "I don't think…I'm too heavy—"

He cut off her words with his mouth, managed to navigate the three steps and placed her on the bed, following her down, desperate to feel her beneath him.

"You're perfect," he said, easing her sweater over her head. "Oh, man."

Appreciating the outline of a woman's breasts against clothing caused a man to fantasize. Unclothed, able to see and touch, was the ultimate fantasy.

He traced the slight swell of her breast above the lace edge of her bra, watched as her stomach dipped on an inhale. Front clasp on the bra, he noted. Promising himself he'd get back to that, he moved his fingers down to the snap of her jeans.

It nearly killed him to say the words, but he had to.

He was ready to explode, but he wouldn't push. "Are you sure?"

Her gaze was steady on his. "Yes. I'm very sure."

In her eyes, he saw trust, and he vowed not to do anything to betray that honor. "I told you I didn't plan this. I'd hoped...so I brought protection."

She covered his hand with hers, subtly urging him to unsnap her jeans, yet at the same time holding him still. "I appreciate that. But I'm on the pill. I have been since I was in my late teens. There are things I should tell you—"

He kissed her before she could continue, tasted the crisp tang of wine on her tongue. He didn't want the past to intrude on the moment. He wanted her total focus on him.

"What came before has nothing to do with now." He meant the words, surprising himself. He didn't care if she'd had a hundred lovers. "You're mine now. That's all that matters."

She wrapped her arms around him, held him with a grip that bordered on desperation. Her breasts pressed against his chest, her scent swirled around him. Had anyone ever held him this close? With this much feeling? He didn't think so. And the power of it, the utter tactile intensity, made his blood heat and his heart ram against his ribs.

Determined to go slow, to savor, he at last unsnapped her jeans, peeled them down her legs. Her panties were a sexy triangle of white lace that matched her bra. The sight of them nearly made him forget his vow not to rush.

"You next," she whispered, reaching for the waist-band of his jeans.

He shook his head. "Not yet. I'm going to take my time with you. I need a little armor, though." If he laid his body to hers, skin to skin, he'd want to be inside her. And then the experience would be over way too soon. They had all night.

And he intended to use every second of the time to devote solely to Victoria Meadland. To make her his. To convince her that there truly weren't any barriers huge enough to keep them apart.

His body was like a furnace, so he whipped off his shirt. And then he satisfied himself by kissing and stroking every inch of her smooth body.

Light from the bedside lamp bathed her alabaster skin in a peachy glow. Her breasts were a perfect handful, her nipples tight and aroused. Two tiny pin-points rode her belly button, an indication it had been pierced but she'd let the holes close up. For some reason, the image of her with a tiny ring in her navel charmed him.

A small, faint band of stretch marks rode both sides of her hips, as though she'd gained weight at some time in her life or gone through a growing spell that her skin couldn't keep up with.

He kissed the marks, felt her go still, traced the slight ridges with the tip of his tongue, and slipped his hands beneath her buttocks, squeezing gently until she surrendered to arousal.

A woman might see these stretch marks as a flaw.

But to Jace, they were simply part of the whole, part of the perfection.

Vickie gripped the sheets of the bed, feeling vulnerable and so incredibly aroused she wasn't sure which emotion to focus on. With his lips, hands and the nearly tangible caress of his gaze, he mapped her body, worshipping, taking his time. She'd never had anyone actually *look* at her this closely, study her with such incredible awe and pleasure. The experience was drugging, thrilling and a little jolting.

The tattoo, she was proud to show off. The stretch marks were another matter entirely.

She should be doing something, she thought, participating. But her limbs wouldn't seem to get her brain's message to cooperate.

In her past experience, sex had been hurried, with a sort of dreaded desperation churning in her belly to get it right, make sure her mate was pleasured, hoping and praying he'd give her time to catch up.

That had rarely happened, but she'd told herself that the power of pleasing a man was what was important. It was what would hold a relationship, lift her above the rest in a man's eyes.

Yet Jace wasn't allowing her a chance to prove her prowess. He stroked her, tasted her, lingered and aroused, complimented her on every part of her body from the crown of her head to the tips of her candy-cane pink toenails.

The friction of denim against her bare legs was its own brand of aphrodisiac, a kind of safety net that guaranteed he wasn't rushing toward his own pleasurable goal line.

And because of that, the urgency of desire grew even hotter. He was pampering her, not expecting anything in return, intent only on her pleasure. She could hardly catch her breath, hold onto a thought. A sweet, steady ache was fast building to an inferno that threatened her control.

When his tongue traced the inside of her thigh, she nearly shot up off the bed. Warm breath feathered against the core of her. Blood rushed through her veins at a momentum that might surely be unhealthy. Exquisitely carnal sensations rolled over her in wave after spine-tingling wave, spiraling her body upward into a climax that slammed through her before she'd even realized it was coming.

Sheer surprise fogged her mind. She might have called out his name, she wasn't sure. She had no idea if the scream in her throat had materialized.

She tugged at his shoulders, reared up to meet him, kissing him, unable to get close enough. "I need to feel your skin. All of you."

Where before the barrier of his jeans was a comfort, now they were a hindrance. She tore at the snaps, rolled with him, nearly sent them over the side of the bed.

"Wait," he said, trying to get his pants kicked off his legs.

"I don't think I can." The moment he'd shed the rest of his clothes, she slid over him, fitted her body to his and tortured them both by rubbing and undulating against him.

Jace cupped her behind, tried to hold her still before he lost his mind. Instead, the firm, steady pressure ground her against his erection in the sweetest form of torture.

Sweat trickled at his temples. He'd meant to call the shots, set the pace, but the sudden frenzy of Vickie's avid lips and remarkable body caught him unaware, stunned him, rendered him motionless for several rapture-filled seconds.

Here was the side of her he'd only seen hints of. The kitten had evolved into an erotic tigress.

With skill and style, her clever mouth sent him to the brink of madness. She matched him, desire for desire. There was genuine enjoyment, unfeigned urgency in her touch.

Exactly the kind of woman a man wanted in his bed.

For the rest of his life.

Finally finding his strength, he rolled with her, positioned her beneath him, gazed down at lake-blue eyes glazed with passion. Something swelled in his chest, an emotion that he had no experience with, had never felt before. An emotion too huge to keep inside.

"I love you." He hadn't known the words were in him, but the instant he whispered them, he knew it was right. She was right. The one for him.

Slowly, carefully, he joined with her, let the power and emotions of his movements speak for him. He thrust into her, each pump of his body punctuating what his heart sang.

Her body clutched him, squeezing and releasing like a gentle fist. She arched beneath him, cried out his name, wrapped her legs around his. The top of his head threatened to explode. He couldn't think. Could only feel.

Somehow, he managed to hold back, unwilling to give her respite just yet. The sense of stunned, erotic wonder on her soft features stroked his ego and fired his blood even hotter.

He took her over the top twice more. Then, with the heady sound of her satisfied cry ringing in his ears, and the pulse of her muscles squeezing, squeezing, squeezing to the throbbing cadence of her heart, he followed her over the edge of bliss.

VICKY HAD TROUBLE catching her breath, making sense of the thoughts that raced through her head. She'd never known that an orgasm was supposed to be like that. Even now, when she should have been sated—*had* been numerous times in this very bed— her body still throbbed with a sweet, greedy ache and she wanted more.

But life-altering sex wasn't the only thing vying for top billing in her mind.

Jace had said he loved her.

She wanted to shout with elation, hug the wonderful feelings to her chest. But she knew that words were often said in the heat of passion that didn't have the weight to carry past the night.

Jace shifted his weight off her, still keeping her close to his side. "I knew it would be like that between us."

"I didn't."

He glanced down at her, a question in his green eyes.

"I've never experienced..." Words failed her. She hadn't known that kind of sex—that kind of making love—existed. "Thank you," she whispered, feeling suddenly close to tears.

He kissed her forehead, giving her a minute to steady. "How about some dessert?"

It took a moment for her mind to switch gears. Perhaps weepy women made him nervous, so he felt the need to distract. "Isn't that what we just had?"

"Mmm. The best." His fingers idly stroked up and down her arm, raising chills on her skin. "The strawberries and champagne I have in the fridge won't even come close. But we could spice them up."

Vivid images of sipping champagne from his incredible body, nibbling sweet berry juice from his lips, sent another fascinating jolt of excitement through her veins. "Got any whipped cream?"

His brows raised. With his customary verve, he swung out of bed. "I'll check."

Although he didn't bother with clothes, seemed perfectly comfortable raiding the kitchen in the nude, Vickie didn't share his confident ease.

She didn't want to get dressed—fully planned to convince him to repeat that fabulous thing he'd done to her navel...and lower—but she felt a little exposed.

Quickly hopping out of bed, she checked the small closet and snatched down one of his button front shirts. The hem hung down to midthigh. She rolled up the long sleeves, sniffed at the fabric. It smelled freshly laundered with a hint of sea air.

She was sitting up in bed, her legs crossed beneath her when he came back. His brows rose.

"I hope you don't think you're going to keep that shirt on for long."

Oh, my gosh. Her stomach leapt into her throat, her heart stuttered and danced. He was magnificent, standing there at perfect ease with himself, his well-developed muscular body looking like a shoo-in candidate for the cover of a men's health magazine.

The intensity of his gaze melted her like hot wax in the sun. She hadn't had an opportunity to really look at him. Now, she had a front row seat...or bunk, rather.

"Um..." She had to shut her gaping mouth before she could form coherent words. "I needed..." *Good grief.* She couldn't string two words together. "I'm modest."

He smiled. "We'll cure you of that." He set a tray on the bed, lifted two crystal goblets and placed them on the nightstand so they wouldn't spill. "But we'll work up to it."

Proving that he understood her hesitation, he stepped into a pair of light blue boxer shorts that sat low on his hips, exposing his navel and the sexy line of dark blond hair that rode his abdomen and fanned upward over his chest.

The mattress dipped as he joined her on the bed, handed her a glass of champagne. With gentle fingers, he traced the curve of her cheek, her jaw, leaned forward and kissed her mouth. It was a tender kiss, filled with a powerful store of emotion.

When she could speak again, she glanced at the tray of berries. "Are we going to eat those strawberries?"

"In a minute."

She couldn't decipher the long look he gave her. It was as though he was worried about something, couldn't make up his mind whether or not to tell her.

Vulnerability, she realized. It was an emotion she'd never have associated with him.

He reached over and lifted his jeans off the floor where he'd thrown them, fished in the pocket and came up with a velvet jewelers box.

Everything within her stilled, then started up again with rushing speed that made her dizzy.

This box wasn't long and flat like the one her bracelet had come it.

It was small. And square.

What in the world had he done now? The sapphire hearts on her bracelet tinkled as she flicked her hair behind her ears, raised her eyes to his.

"Now, this, I *did* plan," he said softly. "Though not exactly in this setting. I had a speech planned out, imagined the ambiance of the stars overhead would add to the romance."

Her heart thundered in her chest. Part in dread, part in giddy anticipation. The dread was because she knew she had no business anticipating in the first place.

He flicked open the lid of the box. "Will you marry me, Victoria?"

Her stunned gaze went from his eyes, to the incredible square-cut diamond engagement ring, then back up. He'd said those words several times before. She'd passed them off as a joke.

This was no joke.

"I..." Tears clogged her throat, filled her eyes. "You don't have to—"

"This isn't because we made love."

It was as though he'd read her mind. She felt a moment of shame for even thinking the thought. Then again, old habits died hard. Another man had once put a ring on her finger—a simulated pearl hardly big enough to see. He'd had no intention of following through on a commitment. He'd only wanted to tie some unhealthy strings to bind her.

"You'll note that I'm paying attention and following advice," Jace said, jolting her back to reality. "I'm told I tend to sweep along and demand. But I'm asking. With my heart and soul."

Sincerity radiated like the steady glow of a morning sunrise. A sincerity that could be believed and counted on.

"I love you, Vickie. Please say yes."

"Yes." The acceptance was out before she could think. She was living the fairy tale. For once, at last, she believed that it was finally her turn for happiness.

He kissed her, took the exquisite solitaire ring from the box and slid it on her finger. All she could do was stare at it in awe.

"It's beautiful," she whispered. The facets of the square-cut gem sparkled in the lamplight. It had to be at least three karats. "But really, Jace. I'll need a bodyguard."

"I'll be your bodyguard." His hands stroked over her shoulders, down her arms, linking together with her fingers. He lifted her hand, kissed her knuckle just above the incredible engagement ring.

"You shouldn't have spent so much money."

"Want me to exchange it?"

She snatched her hand back, closed her fingers into a fist. "No, thank you," she said primly, causing him to laugh and envelope her in an embrace that promised forever.

"Let's toast our future," he suggested, releasing her to retrieve their glasses of champagne from the bedside table.

With the delicate crystal rims touching, his eyes steady on hers, he said softly, "To us."

He'd told her he loved her, asked her to marry him, yet he hadn't pressed her to return the words of love. He was a man who gave so much, didn't guilt someone into giving back more than they were ready for.

A patient man. A very unique man. So perfect it scared her to death.

What if the proverbial other shoe dropped, shattered her idealistic bubble? There were things she hadn't told him. Information he had a right to know.

Things that might well change his mind about her.

With her champagne glass still touching his, her

gaze still locked onto his, she said, "You haven't asked."

He didn't say anything, just patiently waited for her to continue.

"I do love you," she whispered, then sipped the tart liquid to seal the toast.

"I know." His voice was equally as soft, his eyes never leaving hers as he drank, then set his glass aside.

"How?"

"It's in your eyes. Your touch. The way you make me feel."

"I'm a little scared."

"It'll pass."

"Are you always so sure?"

"Always."

She leaned over him, set her glass beside his on the table, took a breath and wondered if she was about to engineer her own doom.

She gazed down at the ring on her finger, a perfect fit. How had he known? "I feel like Cinderella."

"Well, then, I'm definitely your prince."

She laughed because he said it as though he meant it literally. "All I need now is a glass slipper."

"I'll buy you one."

She placed her hand on his thigh. She couldn't stall anymore. Laying bare the mistakes she'd made over the years still caused her a wash of embarrassment. They were stories she found nearly impossible to tell. But it was necessary.

"Jace...there are things I need to tell you. My life hasn't been—"

He pressed a finger to her lips. "Shh. None of that's important. Only now counts. There's nothing you could tell me that would make a difference in how I feel about you."

"How can you be so sure?" Part of her was vastly relieved that he'd let her off the hook. The other part of her was frustrated. Sooner or later, she'd have to make him listen.

"I just am." He reached for her, framed her face in his hands, kissed her in a way that left no doubt he truly believed she was the only woman for him.

"There's a lovers' moon out tonight." He eased her down on the bed, slowly unbuttoned the front of her shirt. "Let's not waste it."

ALTHOUGH THEY'D spent half the night making love, Jace was up by sunrise, exuding so much energy that Vickie felt honor bound to drag herself out of bed and see if she could get into the spirit of being an early riser.

"Sorry, I didn't mean to wake you," he said, pulling a Virginia Tech sweatshirt over his head. "I was trying to be quiet."

She glanced at her watch, her stomach jolting when she saw the unfamiliar diamond ring on her left finger. "Your cheerfulness makes a racket."

"It's called a zest for life," he said with laughter in his eyes. "The sun's shining, I get to drag out my Dracula costume this coming week, and I'm engaged to marry the most beautiful woman on the planet. As long as you're up, though, what do you say we head back in, grab some breakfast and run over to my parents' house and tell them the good news.''

All this "zest" was exhausting. Especially operating on scant hours of sleep. And she'd nearly forgotten they were still anchored in a sheltered cove off the coast. The call of gulls and gentle lap of water against the hull of the boat was both soothing and invigorating.

"Do your parents get up at the crack of dawn, too?"

"Sure. But it won't be the crack of dawn by the time we dock and eat."

She suddenly realized she had a dilemma. "I don't have anything to wear." Jace had a closet full of extra clothes he could change into, but none of them would fit her or be presentable enough to wear to his parents' house without fairly shouting what they'd been doing last night.

"Just put on what you wore yesterday."

"They're wrinkled."

He grinned, scooped her outfit off the floor where he'd tossed it in the heat of passion. "Guess somebody was preoccupied and forgot to hang them up."

The sexy look he gave her thrilled her right down to her toes. "I didn't mind the preoccupation."

He eased onto the side of the bed, nibbled at her jaw, sketched his lips over the incredibly sensitive side of her neck. "We can swing by your place so you can change."

"I'd feel better." Her bones were turning to pudding.

"In the meantime," he said, tugging off his sweatshirt, laying her back and following her down, "no sense in starting the day quite so early. I've a mind to see if I can make that tattoo quiver."

She giggled, then sucked in a breath. Dear heaven, she'd never known the muscles in the small of a woman's back could actually quiver.

Chapter Seven

It was midmorning before they'd returned the boat to the marina and made it to Vickie's apartment for a change of clothes. It was midafternoon before they arrived at his parents house in La Jolla.

The Carradigne driveway was crowded with limousines and official-looking sedans with blacked out windows and flags flying. It looked like the president was visiting. Which wasn't far off the mark. Jace recognized the silver and blue coat of arms on the flags adorning the vehicles.

Jace and his father both owned platinum shields with that same coat of arms.

From Strength, Peace and Independence.

"It looks like your mom and dad have company," Vickie said. "Maybe we shouldn't intrude."

"We're already here. Besides, if mom found out I'd waited even a day to tell them, she'd skin me alive." He parked the Porsche beside the other black cars, secretly pleased that it could easily hold its own among the pack. His Porsche could definitely outrun anything these big lugs had under the hood—if someone cared to race him.

"I don't think your mother's into collecting the skins of her offspring."

He opened her car door for her, took her hand and helped her out. "Don't be too sure. She's scary when she's upset."

He shuddered dramatically and she laughed. He loved the sound of it, loved that she was loosening up, indulging in that laughter more and more. It bothered him when she withdrew behind that wall she often erected. He could only imagine what her growing-up years had been like, being shoved between orphanages as though she were a file of papers nobody knew what to do with.

From now on, she'd always know that she was special. Nothing and no one would hurt her ever again. He'd see to it.

With his arm around her waist, he led her into the house. He heard voices coming from the backyard. "Sounds like they're on the patio."

"I really feel uncomfortable about barging in like this."

"We're not barging. Hell, Mom would set a place at the table for a thief if he happened to stroll in at dinnertime."

"Now you're exaggerating."

"Only a little. You'll see."

Annie Carradigne put her hand on her husband's arm and everyone at the patio table looked up as Jace led Vickie outside.

"You're here," Annie said with relief. "Honestly. You own more communication gadgets than the law allows and don't bother to answer them."

"Did you call?" He'd turned off his phone yesterday and hadn't bothered to check his messages this morning, determined that nothing interfere with his plans for the weekend with Vickie. Monday morning was soon enough to put out any business fires that might arise. If it was serious, he had a highly trained staff that could handle a crisis just as well as he could.

Even as the CEO of Carracell Inc., he was fairly expendable. He'd deliberately made it that way.

"Yes, I called," Annie said. "But you're here now and that's fine. I wanted to introduce you to some of your relatives."

An older man stood, and a swarm of serious-looking bodyguard-types wearing dark coats and sunglasses came to attention like soldiers responding to a drill sergeant's command. Jace's sister, Kelly, looked up from the napkin she was doodling on, and frowned at all the formal hoopla.

"This is His Royal Highness, King Easton Carradigne of Korosol. And this is one of his goddaughters, Miriam Kerr."

The young woman stood, hands clasped at her waist and executed a slight bow. "My great-grandfather was the royal advisor to the king's father during his rule."

Jace nodded, and turned his attention back to the tall, commanding man whose green eyes so like his own held sharp intelligence. This was a man who would make snap decisions and usually be right on target, the kind of man Jace would have hired on the spot regardless of his age.

The king held out his hand. "I am your great-uncle. It is a pleasure to finally meet you, Jace. I have heard nothing but good things about you." He gazed at Vickie, his expression kind. "And who is this?"

"Oh, I'm so sorry," Annie said, all but wringing her hands. The nerves weren't in character. "I'm a bit rattled."

"It's okay, Mom," Jace said. "I came by to tell you all something, but this is even better. More family members present to hear our good news."

"Jace," Vickie whispered. My God, there was a *king* standing in front of them. You didn't just barge in on a *king!* Surely there was protocol. "Maybe this isn't such a great time—"

"It's the perfect time." He turned back to the older man standing so tall and regal, his features pleasant, yet shrewd and watchful. "Your Highness—"

"Call me Easton."

"Easton, then. This is Victoria Meadland." He swept his gaze around the table, including the rest of his family. "Everybody, I've asked Vickie to marry me, and she said yes." He held her close, pressed a kiss to her temple.

Annie was the first to jump up and hug Vickie, including Jace in the embrace.

Chris joined his wife. "Turn loose of your fiancée, son, so we can welcome her properly."

Jace did as he was told and Chris enveloped her in

a warm hug. "Welcome to the family, Victoria. First off, I've got to know. Did he ask or tell you?"

Vickie glanced at the king, who was smiling now. The bodyguards hovering close by were as solemn as henchmen. Lord, what had she gotten herself into? Never in her wildest dreams...

Chris had asked her a question, she remembered. Ask or tell. Obviously Chris knew his son's steam-roller tactics well.

She looked over at Jace, and every face in the room, royal or otherwise, faded from her mind. All the love in her heart had to be beaming from her eyes. "He asked."

After she'd showed off her ring, and received a shy congratulations from Kelly, Chris clapped his son on the back, shook hands, then pulled him into an embrace. "Nice to know you paid attention to your old man."

"I imagine Vickie could tumble my image if she wanted to."

Chris glanced at Vickie, raised his sandy brows. Father and son looked so much alike, open, friendly, dynamic and happy. This is what Jace would look like in twenty-five years. A clone of Robert Redford. How in the world had she gotten so lucky?

She shook her head at Chris's inquiry, smiled softly. "He's perfect."

Jace laughed and swept her off her feet, twirling them around. "Is she great or what?" Setting her down, her head spinning, he said softly, "And she's mine."

Then, in front of an entire audience—a good many of them royalty—he kissed her. Softly, tenderly, lovingly. It made her eyes sting with tears. Tears of joy, of disbelief. That this perfect man loved her. Wanted her.

Forever.

When someone cleared their throat, Vickie pulled away, felt her face heat. Jace kept his arm around her, held her close to his side in a gesture that seemed to say if anyone had any objection, it was too darn bad.

That alone touched her more deeply than anything else had in her life. She'd never had a champion, never been made to feel so accepted. By a man. Or by a family.

The experience was heady.

"You'll have to forgive us, Easton," Chris said. "This is the first wedding in our immediate family, and we're understandably excited. Especially over adding Vickie to the clan."

"That is quite all right," the king said, his laughter so like Jace's. Vickie imagined that the people of his kingdom adored him. "I am enjoying myself immensely."

"Why don't we all go into the living room and sit down," Annie said. "Jace, Easton has come to talk with the family, and I think we should get comfortable."

Linking hands with Vickie, he followed his parents and King Easton into the formal room reserved for company. Since this was royal company, it seemed necessary.

The king's entourage stood just inside the doors, respectfully declining a seat. One of the men carrying a cell phone stepped outside, presumably to conduct royal business.

The only one who joined the group was Miriam Kerr, the King's goddaughter. Young, probably not yet even twenty-five, she was extremely proper. Stylish business suit, low-heeled pumps, ankles crossed and tucked just so, hands clasped lightly in her lap. Her makeup was flawless, her skin perfumed ever so subtly.

In the way of a lifelong king used to being center stage, Easton chose to stand in front of the group. He studied the faces around him, pleased with what he saw. Christopher Carradigne's offspring were both quite impressive. Much more impressive than some in the family tree.

Jace especially intrigued him. The boy had a head for business, had made his first million just two years out of college and had kept right on building his fortune. He was the wisest choice. Optimistic, easygoing, sense of humor, yet a commanding leader. His education and background were impeccable. Christopher and Annie had done an excellent parenting job here.

Kelly, on the other hand, had intelligence as well. A child prodigy, already a scientist at age twenty-six. He couldn't wait to discuss her research in depth, research he'd been privately, anonymously funding. He fully intended to lend himself as her test subject—for the drug she'd recently developed could well prolong his life.

She was a shy little mouse, though. Oh, she had a good heart, and would move mountains to help those in need, but he wasn't quite sure what to make of her. Even now, she appeared preoccupied, staring at some complex mathematical figures she'd scribbled on a napkin.

She also had an odd habit of muttering to herself. Twice today, he'd stopped talking, certain she was attempting to interrupt him—something few people dared in his presence. Even now, *especially* now, it was disconcerting not to have her full attention, yet he imagined if he put her on the spot, she'd look up from her complicated equations and repeat the last five spoken sentences verbatim.

She was the spitting image of his dearly departed sister, Magdalene. Just looking at her made his heart ache. The people of Korosol would notice the resemblance as well, and that could count as a plus.

Still, Jace was his best choice. And time was of the essence. He was desperate to name an heir to the throne, to protect the people of his country that he would willingly lay down his life for. What life he had left, that is.

"I've invited myself to your home to impose on your hospitality, Christopher, for a very important mission."

"Family is never an imposition," Chris said. "You're always welcome."

"Thank you. It's come the time that I'm forced to accept that I must step down from the throne, thus, I have a rather pressing need to name my heir. It is our custom that I may ignore birth order if I choose and appoint the heir of my choice.'' He had everyone's complete attention now—including Kelly's.

He settled his gaze on Jace. ''You are ninth in line to the crown, Jace. And you, Kelly are tenth. It is my wish, Jace, after careful evaluation, that you would do myself and our country the honor of accepting your duty by succeeding me as the king of Korosol. You have the virtues of a leader and the compassion of a friend. Both qualities that I, myself, possess and admire.''

Dead silence reigned for several moments. Jace looked around the room, stunned into speechlessness. Four sets of eyes besides his own were agog. Only Miriam and Easton remained passive.

Finding his voice, he said, ''Whoa. What about the other eight before me?''

''I have spoken to them. Your second cousins in New York—delightful princesses, all of them—feel they are not at a point in their lives to rule our country, nor do they choose to. CeCe and her husband, Shane O'Connell, have recently become the proud parents of a fine and healthy son. Amelia, somewhat of a danger seeker, that one, has settled down to raise the two precious children she and her husband, Nicholas Standish, have adopted, and she happily informed me she's in the family way. Lucia, recently married to one of my retired generals, wants to concentrate on marriage and is reluctant to live in the spotlight.''

There was fondness and respect as he spoke about each of his granddaughters, but a subtle thread of anxiety bled through as he explained how each had turned him down.

Vickie was fascinated listening to him, watching his expressions. He struck her as a man who'd spent his life doing exactly as he wished. And he reminded her so much of Jace. Except, where Jace was tanned and the picture of health, Easton appeared a bit pale, as though he'd recently suffered a bout of illness.

"Next, I spent four months with your cousins in Wyoming," Easton continued, "trying to determine if any of the men were right for the position of king. But they all had their own problems to deal with and their own lives to lead. One by one, they each turned me down. As I said, I will not force any of you, and accepting the crown is no light obligation. But I would hope the blood of our ancestors, *my* blood, runs in one of you for the love of our countrymen."

His gaze touched on Kelly, who was staring at him like a deer caught in the headlights of a hunter's vehicle. Then he turned his attention back to Jace.

"One of you with leadership skills, a sense of honor, duty and integrity. You, Jace, are next in line. You are the blood of my sister, and she was all of those qualities and more."

Vickie shifted in her seat, discreetly glanced at her watch, both fascinated and overwhelmed by what she was hearing. King Easton had just described Jace down to the bone. And she could see by the rapt expression on Jace's face that the idea intrigued him. Where Kelly seemed to be trying to disappear in hopes she'd escape the king's notice, Jace appeared energized, excitement radiating from him.

He'd told her himself that his business could survive without him, that if he had the opportunity to get his teeth into a new and exciting endeavor, he'd jump at the chance.

This appointment was right up his alley. He would be perfect.

And, oh, my goodness, she wouldn't just be a princess, Vickie realized. As his wife, she would be a queen. It was too much to think about. Especially since she was due to be at work in a couple of hours.

"I need some time to absorb all of this," Jace said. "And I've got so many questions about Korosol. I'm trying to put them in order."

"It would be best if we could sit down, the two of us and answer those questions."

Jace glanced down at Vickie, which gave her the opportunity to interrupt without appearing rude. He was in the middle of a life-altering meeting and she didn't want to take him away from it.

Still, she had a job and people counting on her. "I need to get to work."

He checked his watch. "I didn't realize it was so late. I'll drive you."

"No. Jace, you need to stay."

He hesitated, clearly torn. "Then take my car." He fished in his pocket for the keys, never even hesitating over turning her loose in his Porsche.

Now *that* was trust.

But ever the planner, Vickie shook her head. "If I take your car, how will you get home?"

"Perhaps I can be of assistance," Easton said. "Do forgive me for listening in on a private conversation. But my driver will be happy to take you wherever you wish to go, Victoria."

It was the best solution. "Thank you. That would be wonderful."

"Are you sure?" Jace asked. "I don't mind taking you."

"Are you kidding? I'm dying to ride in that fancy limousine."

He laughed and walked with her out to the car. When she slid into the luxurious, buttery leather seat and stared around in wonder, he chuckled.

"Get used to it. There's a good possibility we could be traveling via this mode quite a bit."

He leaned in the door and gave her a lingering kiss, then stood back as the driver pulled away from the Carradigne grounds.

Vickie felt as giddy as a teenager on the way to the prom. The day's events were simply too much to take in at once.

She was engaged to a prince. *A prince!*

That Cinderella thing was starting to take on a heck of a lot of meaning—and there wasn't a mean step-mother in sight.

THE HOTEL DEL CORONADO was reputed to be the best in the city, which is why he'd chosen to stay there. He deserved the best, *insisted* on it.

He glanced across the room to the woman pawing through hotel stationery and slipping memorabilia into her oversize tote bag. She was older than him by five years—he suspected it might be even more—but her five-foot-three figure was still curvy and her sleek, jet-black hair gave her the appearance of sophistication.

She was a journalist—if you could call it that—and had her own gossip column on page seven of the *Manhattan Chronicle*. Pushy, she'd get her stories any way she could. He liked that about her, found her useful for his purposes. In some ways, they were two of a kind, unwilling to let anyone get in the way of what they wanted.

They were having an affair—that, too, he found useful. She was pretty decent in bed, but that wasn't the main link between them as far as he was concerned. The primary passion they shared had to do with the Carradignes.

He fed her information, she made it public. He figured she owed him plenty. Because of him, she'd scooped all the other journalists and shocked the city of New York with a juicy story on the East Coast branch of the mighty Carradigne dynasty.

The public had eaten it up, and her column had been syndicated. Quite a handy promotion seeing as he now had this latest piece of business on the West Coast.

He lifted the glass of fine scotch to his lips, sipped, felt a pleasant buzz. The old man had accused him of being an alcoholic. What a crock, he thought, rubbing a belly that had begun to expand over the past few years. He'd pit his mind against that decrepit has-been any day of the week.

When his cell phone rang, he idly punched the talk button. "Speak," he commanded, getting a thrill at knowing his order would be obeyed.

"He has asked Jace Carradigne to be his heir," the man on the other line said, his accent thick.

"Did he accept?"

"Not yet. There is a new development. The girl-friend is now a fiancée."

He felt his juices starting to flow, his mind racing with possibilities. "Did you get what I asked for?"

"Her name is Victoria Meadland, sir. She is a cock-tail waitress at a local bar. I think you'll find the rest of my information very beneficial."

"You know what to do."

"Yes, sir."

He hung up the phone, gazed at a pair of nicely shaped legs in his line of vision, felt his body stir with desire. Being on a quest never failed to turn him on.

"Well?" she asked.

"Come here." He pulled her down in his lap, pressed her hand over his straining erection. "We might be able to do this the clean way. My oh-so-perfect cousin has gotten himself engaged. Seems there might be more than a speck of scandal in the lucky girl's past, which could prove sad for young Carradigne. Korosol, and the old man for that matter, are sticklers for pristine backgrounds."

She rubbed against him, smiled slowly, her ruby lips

moist from where she'd licked them. "How long before we get the details?"

"Two hours, tops."

"And then what?"

"Someone will convince her it would be best to get out of town. Lover boy will follow her, of course. He'll realize that accepting the kingdom will jeopardize his lady love and do the right thing. And the old man will be left once again without a willing heir."

"You're placing a lot of faith on the strength of Jace Carradigne's feelings."

"It's a gamble. But I'm a betting man. And I think it'll pay off. We've got nothing on him, so we'll hit him where he's vulnerable. Through his lady."

"And if it doesn't work?"

Anger boiled that she'd question him. "Then we'll go to plan B."

She seemed to realize she'd stepped over the line. Her hands slid deeper between his legs, mollifying him for the moment.

"You're going to make me famous," she purred.

"Yes. And you'll help make me king."

ONCE TIFFANY spied Vickie's ring, there was no keeping the engagement a secret. Not that she'd wanted to, but with the king's arrival and this latest news, doubts were nagging, trying to crowd in and burst her euphoric bubble.

"Good God. That's a rock if I ever saw one. What is it, ten karats?" Tiffany asked.

"I think it's three."

"You *think?* Girl, when a man gives you a diamond it's your duty as a female to find out the size, color, clarity and price tag—right down to the tiniest fraction!"

"You are so hung up on dollar signs."

"And I never deny it. See that gentleman over there at table eight? I've got my eye on him. He's wearing a genuine Rolex watch. I can tell the difference between the real thing and a knockoff from fifty paces. He's got a fine body to go with that wad of dough he flashed a few minutes ago. Ordered a gin and tonic with lime, tipped me a hundred bucks and asked me to come get to know him on my break." She glanced at her own watch, which was flashy, but surrounded with cut crystal rather than the real thing.

"I'm due in five minutes. Can you cover me if I go over?"

Vickie smiled. "I'm a woman in love. Of course I'll cover for you."

"Thanks, hon. You're a peach. Wish me luck. Maybe we'll both land in some tall clover."

Vickie just shook her head and picked up her pace. There had been a mix-up with the band scheduled to play tonight, so it was quieter than usual for a Saturday night. The lack of entertainment had cut their clientele by a third.

She served drinks, wiped tables, flirted with a couple of happily soused businessmen and flashed her diamond ring to let them know she was taken. Each time she thought about it, she felt giddy.

A genuine prince. And she was engaged to marry him.

What would good old Helen the Horrible think if she saw her now? Vickie had an unholy urge to drop in on the group home. She'd be wearing a suit made of the finest silk, sensible shoes—one shouldn't have their toes pinched regardless of fashion—and perhaps she'd carry a Prada bag. Heck, she might as well wear a small, tasteful tiara while she was at it. She'd arrive in an elegant limo, and she'd have Jace at her side. Tall and commanding, her golden-haired prince would lend her the strength and credibility she hadn't been able to muster all those years ago.

Instead of sniffing as though she'd smelled something foul, Helen would choke on the wad of gum she habitually chewed like a cow gorging on cud.

"Well," Tiffany said, breezing up to the bar as though she'd been working all along. "I finally meet Mr. Right, and all he wants to talk about is you."

"Me? Why?"

"Because you're a dish. Don't you look in the mirror?"

"I'm sorry."

"Cut it out, hon. You can't help it that you're a walking fantasy. Wholesome and sexy all in one. I told him you were happily engaged, and that brought his attention back around to me. You'll forgive me, but I had to make you sound like you weren't such a great catch." Tiffany patted Vickie's arm. "With a guy like that, though, I don't mind being second choice. His name's Esteban—he told me to call him Steven—and he runs an import-export business in Spain. He's taking me out to dinner after my shift.''

''Good for you. Just be careful, Tiff. You don't know this guy.''

''I know enough.'' She laughed. ''And I intend to know a lot more.''

Vickie knew better than to worry about Tiffany. The woman always landed on her feet.

The rest of her shift passed quickly, although she kept watching the door, half-expecting Jace to come strolling in like he usually did. But she understood that he had a huge decision to make, decades worth of knowledge to catch up on.

When she got home, she fed Sissy, showed off her diamond ring—which the cat didn't seem overly impressed by—then literally fell into bed. She hadn't had much sleep the night before and it had caught up with her.

She woke up at six o'clock the next morning, still wearing her clothes. Jace was a bad influence on her. Or maybe it was good. She hadn't been up before seven-thirty on a Sunday morning in years.

Heading for the coffeepot, she poured a cup, then stepped outside for the newspaper. A caption in a small box in the lower corner caught her eye.

Millionaire Cell Phone Magnate Named Prince. Could There Be Wedding Bells In The Future For This Prince Charming? See Article On Page Seven.

Vickie nearly spilled her coffee as she snatched at the pages, looking for the article.

Krissy Katwell was the name on the byline. It was

a gossip column, and two-thirds of it was devoted to Jace and the success he'd made by building his company from the ground up.

A brief synopsis told of his connection to the royal family of Korosol and speculated as to whether or not this eligible bachelor would be named the next heir to the throne.

Katwell went on to tease the reader by posing the question: Will our Prince Charming remain the most eligible bachelor or will hearts break all over the nation? Sources hint that there could be wedding bells in his future. Stay tuned for further developments on who this mystery woman might be.

Feeling overwhelmed, Vickie sat down and rested her head in her palm. What had she done? She was engaged to a man who's lineage made it a given that their life would be lived in a fishbowl.

The media could be both a blessing and a curse. If a person was the slightest bit newsworthy, salivating journalists considered it their duty to ferret out their secrets and tell the world.

The article in front of her proved that Jace was already newsworthy.

The phone rang and she was sure it was Jace. She needed time to think, but she needed to hear his voice even more. Her fairy tale was crumbling at the edges. Jace held the glue.

"Hello?"

"Victoria Meadland?"

It was a man's voice. One she didn't recognize.

"Yes."

"The Victoria Meadland whose ex-boyfriend is doing time in the Oregon State Prison?"

Chills raced up her spine. A jolt of adrenaline made pinpoints of light dance before her eyes. Oh, dear God. It was starting. "Who is this?"

"That's not important. What's important is if Krissy Katwell digs up your past and prints it, there'll be a feeding frenzy among every gossip rag in the country. You haven't been a very good little girl, have you, Vickie?"

"I don't know who this is, but you're sick if you get your kicks making this kind of phone call. I'm—"

"You'd be stupid to hang up on me. I hate it when that happens, and I'm not someone you'll want to anger."

Fear was like a living beast inside her, but as much as she wanted to, she couldn't bring herself to slam down the phone.

He knew about Darren. She had to know what this was all about. Otherwise, she'd be a basket case wondering, jumping at shadows when she had no idea if there were even shadows she should be jumping at.

"What do you want?"

"To see your apartment empty and you out of town. Permanently."

"Why?"

"Because you're not princess material."

The comment cut her to the quick. For an instant, her mind flashed back to the orphanage, a little girl cowering in the corner. *You come from white trash and that's all you'll ever be.* Her sweaty palm tightened on the receiver.

"If you stay, you'll be fodder for the news," the man continued. "Being associated with the Carradignes will put you in the headlines. And that Katwell woman will dig until she knows every last bit of dirt on you. Little by little, you'll ruin the prince's image in his people's eyes. They'll never accept you—a woman who shacked up with a jailbird. And because of you, they won't accept him. Decide if you want that weight on your conscience. You've got twenty-four hours." The line went dead.

Trembling so bad she could hardly hang up the phone, Vickie stooped down and lifted Sissy in her arms. Protective instincts or needing to be consoled, she wasn't sure. The cat purred, for once didn't object to being squeezed.

Vickie paced as thoughts whirled. She thought of Darren Hawkins sitting in a prison cell wearing an orange jumpsuit, smoking a cigarette, his long hair pulled into a ponytail.

Darren knows about the baby.

"Oh, God." Bile churned in her stomach as the familiar shame nearly bent her double. Since she'd testified against Darren during his drug-trafficking trial, there was no love lost between the two of them. He'd be more than happy to spill secrets she'd foolishly told him in confidence.

Now, not only was she jeopardizing Jace's reputation and opportunity to accept his rightful heritage, a child's security and way of life was at stake. A child who hadn't asked for any of this, who was the innocent.

A child Vickie had borne and given up for adoption when she was sixteen.

She twisted the sapphire rings on her fingers. Her birthstone. And her daughter's.

The decision she made nearly ripped her heart out. But it was an easy one.

The lives of the two people she loved most in the world were at stake. Because of her.

Chapter Eight

Jace had been cooped up at his parents' house and had only managed a bit of freedom when he'd told everyone he had urgent business to see to at his company.

That didn't stop Sir Devon Montcalm, Captain of Korosol's Royal Guard, from shadowing him. Every time he turned around, the solemn, well-built, by-the-book guy was there. If a person was used to this sort of thing, it would be okay. But for Jace, who'd been captain of the wrestling team in college and was no slouch in the fist department if the situation was unavoidable, the very idea of someone thinking he needed his body guarded pricked at his ego.

This utter lack of privacy gave him a few doubts about what his great-uncle was urging him to do. Hell, he hadn't considered himself a possible heir to the throne. Ninth in line was pretty low on the food chain. Besides, he'd never even set foot on Korosolan soil.

But he was a man who loved a challenge, and this new venture, the idea of being a king, appealed to him. More than he'd realized it would.

Plus, his uncle had confided that he had a rare heart disease. His days were numbered. He was desperate to know he had the right successor before the inevitable happened.

That had just about cinched it for Jace. Family had always been important to him, and family duty was something he never shirked. Even though he'd never been to Korosol, it was his heritage, his roots. Aside from the family draw, though, was the excitement he felt toward a new project, like the barely contained excitement he'd experienced when first going into business for himself. He'd taken Carracell Inc. to the top. This was the perfect time in his life to dig his teeth into something new.

But Vickie had a stake in his decision, and he couldn't, *wouldn't* make it without her.

Anxious to see her, knowing he had Sir Devon on his tail, he put the Porsche in gear and wound it out, grinning when the distance between his taillights and the black sedan lengthened. Oh, he figured the guy would eventually catch up, but he might as well make him work for it.

Vickie's car wasn't on the street when he parked in front of her apartment. She should have been home from school by now. She was due to work at Diamond Jim's tonight, but since he hadn't seen her in almost forty-eight hours, he was restless and impatient.

He'd called yesterday, but she'd told him she had a migraine and just needed to rest. And since Easton, his closest advisors and Miriam Kerr had been buzzing around him like bees on a honeycomb, firing information and instruction on protocol faster than he could keep up, he'd stayed away for the day.

But he was worried about her, because when he'd called this morning before she left for school, she hadn't sounded good.

He should have put everyone else on hold, gone to her yesterday regardless of her insistence that she'd be fine, taken care of her, rubbed her head, made her chicken soup.

By damn, if she was sick, he wasn't letting her stand on her feet half the night serving Monday night drinkers. This was her usual night off, but Paul had told him last week that a computer convention would be in town this week, and that Vickie would be working her days off. That's why he'd so readily agreed to the night off on Friday so Jace could propose.

He'd been knocking on her front door for several minutes before he saw Devon's car pull into a parking spot a half a block away. He smirked.

When Vickie didn't answer the door, he took out his cell phone and punched the preprogrammed button for her apartment. He could hear the phone ringing, both in his ear and through the door. He counted thirty rings before he disconnected. No answer. Not even a message machine with her sweet voice inviting him to express his worry.

The blinds were closed and Sissy wasn't roaming outside. He walked around the apartment complex, checked the parking structure, keeping his eye out for the cat.

He tried Diamond Jim's, but Paul said she wasn't

there yet, didn't expect her until six. At least he still expected her.

For some reason that didn't give him much comfort. Maybe she was studying in the library. It was a logical explanation, but a bad feeling was sitting in the pit of his stomach.

Vickie was punctual. Like clockwork. He'd never known her to deviate from her routine.

He pressed the automatic dial and paced until his mother picked up the phone. "Mom? Can you do me a favor? Call over to San Diego State and see if Vickie showed up for classes today?"

"What's wrong, honey?"

"Probably nothing. I'm just having trouble locating her and she wasn't feeling good yesterday."

Annie sighed. "Aren't we being a little impatient?"

"Can you do it?" His gut twisted tighter.

"Yes. I know some people. I'll call you right back."

Devon had gotten out of the car by now and was approaching from the sidewalk. About five years younger than him, the guy was built like a tank. His carriage shouted military with a capital *M*.

"Problem?" Devon asked.

"I don't know." His cell phone rang. He glanced at the caller identification, nearly bobbled the instrument getting it to his ear. "Was she there?"

"No. Honey, she didn't go to any of her classes today. What's going on?"

"I don't know," he repeated, his gaze meeting

Devon's. "I'll check in with you later, Mom. Thanks for making the call."

He disconnected, paced. Fear was whipping into full-blown panic.

"You're having trouble locating Ms. Meadland?"

"Yes. I've tried the apartment, school and work. Nobody's seen her."

"When was the last time you talked to her?"

"This morning before she left for school—except I just found out she never showed up for classes. Damn it, I don't like this. It doesn't feel right." He stared at the tiny phone in his hand. "She doesn't even carry a cell phone. What kind of person doesn't carry a cell phone?" he demanded to no one in particular.

"Your fiancée?" Devon said with little expression.

He stopped pacing, shot him a you're-not-helping look.

Devon shrugged, turned his back and made a phone call. When he disconnected, he said to Jace, "I'll check around. See what I can come up with."

The man was short on words and didn't waste time. He merely turned and walked away. Jace didn't like the thoughts that were crowding in. Like why would the Captain of the Royal Guard volunteer so quickly to locate Vickie's whereabouts—especially since he'd asked very few questions.

It was way too early in the game to consider this a crisis, no matter what his gut was trying to tell him otherwise.

AFTER DEVON left, Jace noticed that another guy in a black sedan had become his shadow. For the sheer hell of it, he decided to give the guy the slip. Obviously, this one wasn't as skilled as Montcalm, because Jace managed to shake him in a matter of minutes.

The Porsche didn't have a beefy engine in it for nothing.

He waited at Diamond Jim's until seven o'clock, but Vickie didn't show up for work. Tiffany and Paul knew even less than he did.

Jace checked all the hospitals in the area, but no one meeting Vickie's description had been admitted. She didn't have any family and the only real friend Jace knew of was Tiffany.

And Tiffany was just as worried as the rest of them. She'd known Vickie the longest and agreed that Vickie wouldn't just disappear without calling.

He headed back toward his condo, hoping she'd be waiting for him there. They could laugh over his panic. If she wasn't there, though, he was going to go back to her apartment and break down the damned door. With or without the manager's permission or presence.

It was late when he got home. Vickie wasn't sitting on his front doorstep as he'd hoped.

His frustration over her not carrying a cell phone was about to eat him alive. Even if she kept it in her purse and didn't turn it on, he could have at least left her a message. Damn it, he should have bought her one. He'd bought her a bracelet and a ring, but not the most important thing—a communication device that she should keep on her person.

He ought to be run clean out of the telecommunications business.

After he put the Porsche in the garage, he went around to the front door to check the mail.

Devon Montcalm materialized out of the dark, scaring the hell out of him.

"Geez, man. Give a guy a heart attack, why don't you?" He snatched the lid on the mail box more forcefully than he'd intended. An envelope fell out.

Devon body-blocked him and got to it first.

"There are laws in this country over tampering with a person's mail," Jace said, fear and panic over the day's events boiling into a healthy steam of anger. He didn't feel the emotion often, but when he did, it was swift and sharp. And right now, he could easily go for a good fight to relieve some of the pressure.

Lecturing himself to calm down, trying to remember the steps of the workshops he taught to his own employees on positive energy flow and overcoming obstacles, he stood back and waited—impatiently—as Devon blithely opened his mail.

"No stamp," Devon said, using a glove he'd taken out of his jacket to hold the edges of the envelope. "And no address. Just your name."

Okay, that was a little strange.

When Devon looked up, Jace didn't like the expression on his face. He took the envelope the other man held out.

The engagement ring nearly fell to the ground when he removed the single sheet of paper.

Devon caught it, glanced at it, handed it back to Jace.

The note wasn't even signed. There were only two words. "I'm sorry."

The first emotion to slam into him was pain. Deep, cutting, agonizing pain. Then disbelief. By God, she hadn't faked her feelings. He'd stake his life on it. Which meant that she was scared about something. The possibility of him being a king?

No, that didn't wash. She yearned for a glass slipper. She'd said it in jest, but he'd heard the wistful longing in her voice.

The only other explanation was that she'd met with foul play. Kidnapping?

He turned to Devon. "What kind of risk does this prince and king position come with?"

"A person in high political standing is never risk free."

"You didn't answer my question. Is there something I should know? I mean, you're sticking to me like flypaper. Would my accepting this title in any way remotely put Vickie in jeopardy?"

"That wouldn't have been one of my great concerns, no. There's always a possibility you could become a target. Like the President of your United States. He is surrounded by Secret Service men."

"And so is the First lady," Jace snapped.

"But not generally a target."

"Not *generally*," Jace stressed. "Damn it. If something's happened to Vickie because of me…"

Devon shifted on his feet, his gaze scanning every

corner of the darkness even though he didn't appear to be doing so.

He nodded at the ring in Jace's hand. "A kidnapper's not likely to return a ring that valuable. Extortion is usually their game."

"What if it's not money they're after?"

"In that hypothetical scenario, you're dealing with criminal, often unstable minds. And people fitting that profile wouldn't let go of a rock like that, even if money wasn't their angle." He paused, his expression never changing. "If that were the case, there'd likely be a finger attached to that ring."

Jace felt his face go pale. He swore, had an overpowering urge to plow his fist into Devon's expressionless face for even planting that image in his mind.

"Has the whole world gone mad? Damn it, this cloak-and-dagger stuff isn't part of my life."

"What I'm trying to say—*delicately*—is that maybe the lady just had a change of heart."

Razor-edged pain slashed at his gut again. He shook his head. "I don't believe it. I know her better. I'm calling the police."

This statement did bring a change in expression. Devon took a step forward, put his hand over the cell phone Jace was raising. Jace felt the vibration of strength in the other man's hold, but knew he could match it.

"I'll handle it," Devon said.

"How? You're only one man. I have the San Diego police department and an entire nation of FBI agents at my disposal. You think you could do better than them?''

''Yes.'' It was said quietly, firmly.

Skepticism was keen, but something in the steady look of the man in front of him made him believe the guy might know what he was talking about.

''Our country has resources and less...red tape than yours does. The local police will take reports, investigate, spend weeks. Even if the Feds are brought in, the case will be slotted. There are no guarantees as to how much priority it'll receive.''

Jace knew what Devon said was true. Vickie wasn't a missing child. Technically, she had no family. He wasn't married to her yet, so his connections and badgering wouldn't count for much. His money could buy the best private investigators, but it couldn't guarantee top priority with the local police or U.S. government.

''Since Ms. Meadland is your intended princess, the Korosol government will leave no stone unturned in locating her. However, I've been concerned that there's a leak in my guard, or among King Easton's advisors. I'd like to handle this personally, with my own chosen team.''

Jace nodded. ''You're hired. Whatever it costs, whatever it takes, just find her.''

''I already have a job and a salary.'' Devon shoved his hands in his pockets. ''You want to invite me inside so I can give you an update on what I know so far?''

Jace unlocked the door. ''I'm a little torn up at the

moment.'' It was the best apology he was going to give for being inhospitable.

''Understandable. Nice view,'' Devon commented, gazing out at the city lights across the bay. ''You might want to draw those drapes.''

The guy didn't break character for a second, Jace thought. ''Do you want a beer?''

''No.'' He let the issue of the drapes go. ''I accessed Ms. Meadland's phone records while you were doing whatever it was you were doing.''

Jace found that he could grin, even under the circumstances. ''That guy sucks at tailing a subject.''

''Yes, well they all can't be as good as me.''

''I checked at Diamond Jim's,'' Jace said, popping the top on a beer. ''Called all the hospitals, went back to her house, the park, every place I could think of.''

''Good. Her phone records indicate she called the landlord of her building—''

''I couldn't get in touch with him. I tried, but he wasn't home.''

''He has his hair cut the last Monday of the month, then bowls on a league. The team meets for pizza before the game. This past weekend he was in Los Angeles for his grandson's birthday party.''

''How do you know all that?''

Devon looked at him as though he was a dim bulb, and simply continued. ''The landlord wasn't much help. Said he opened his door this morning and her potted plants and flowers were on his doorstep. The apartment came furnished so there wouldn't have been a need for a moving company. Personal belongings are gone, place is clean as a whistle. She'd paid first and last month's rent and wasn't bound by a lease, so he's not out any money. Just sad to have a good tenant leave."

The beer tasted like cardboard, but he sipped anyway. Maybe it would dull this ache inside. Why did he feel as though there'd been a death in the family?

The thought blindsided him. He firmly put a stop to that line of thinking.

"She also called the telephone and utility companies," Devon said. "As well as San Diego State University. She withdrew from all of her classes—the counselor I spoke with said that's the smart thing to do if you find you can't attend. Otherwise you'd get F's in each class and it lowers the grade point average considerably."

"School was everything to her," Jace said. "She wouldn't sacrifice an entire semester just to break an engagement. She's a hell of a lot tougher than that."

Devon glanced back down at his notes, didn't comment. "Incoming calls were mainly from your various numbers—home, work, cell, parents."

"How does someone just leave without a trail?"

"There's usually a trail. It's a matter of finding it. However, you said she ran away from an orphanage at sixteen, and that she's tough. Someone with that background knows how to lay low, travel light."

Jace's stomach dipped. Images he didn't want to examine flashed in his mind. Images of a young girl, alone and scared, only herself to rely on. A young girl with no safe haven to run to.

"There was another incoming call on record. Made Sunday morning, 7:12 a.m. from a phone booth in the city. Strikes me as odd, because a scrambling device was employed, similar to the equipment we use in Korosol for sensitive operations. It's next to impossible to trace."

"Did you forget what business I'm in?"

"You're a suit, Jace. That's been your main function for the past few years. Besides, I know for a fact that no one in the United States has a system that can crack this code. I designed it and I've tried."

"Okay, you said *next* to impossible, but not impossible."

Devon nodded. "It'll take a while. It'd be easier if I was in Korosol. My computer usually networks with the mainframe but I've got a glitch."

"Are glitches the norm?"

"No."

In other words, Jace thought, someone didn't want Devon tracing the call that was made to Vickie. Panic tried to claw at his belly again.

"So what are you waiting for? Take my jet and go straighten out the snag."

"I'm assigned to guard you and the king."

"To hell with me. I don't need a shadow. And Easton's got enough puppets to guard an army."

Devon's lips canted but he didn't actually smile. "You gave one of those puppets the slip today."

"Guess you need to bone up on your training skills, Captain."

"Guess I do. I'll take the Korosol jet. It'll be faster."

Now *that* was both an affront and a challenge. Jace's jet was top of the line. He'd made sure of it. However…

He picked up his cell phone, finger hovering over the key pad. "Are there any royal rules prohibiting security guys from flying the Concorde?"

Devon broke character for a flash of an instant and smiled. "Money."

"Then we have no problem. This'll be on my dime."

IT HAD BEEN a month and still no word on Vickie. Jace's concentration was the pits. Although Easton had given Devon the go-ahead to devote his time and effort to finding Vickie, he'd urged Jace to move forward in his lessons on the varied protocol of their country, claiming it would keep his mind busy.

Jace had reluctantly agreed. He still hadn't given his final answer on being appointed Easton's heir. His future was with Vickie and she had a say in it as well.

He had to hold on to that hope.

Miriam Kerr, ever the proper little thing, was fussing around him, instructing the tailors on fitting him in yet *another* tuxedo. His peaceful condo had been turned into a circus—bodyguards standing like soldiers at the doors and windows, secretaries arranging fancy evenings out. He'd put his foot down at meeting government officials, because he still hadn't agreed to this gig.

"This is bogus. I've got tuxedos in my closet that cost more than most people earn in a month. Why do I need so many more?"

"These have the Korosol crest."

"So sew one of the damn things on the pocket of mine."

Miriam snatched the material at his waist, nearly strangling the breath out of him. "Another tuck here, Armand," she said pleasantly.

Jace glared at her. She'd done that on purpose. The fit was just fine. "That secretary's wasting her time, you know. I'm not attending the opera. I hate opera. What would it look like anyway if people knew I was representing your country—"

"*Your* country, too," Miriam amended.

"—and I started snoring?"

"That would be poor form, indeed."

He checked his watch and Armand sighed when his chalk mark for an alteration went awry.

"Are we done yet?"

"Finished," Miriam corrected.

"Yes," Armand said with a great deal of relief.

"Good. I need a beer. Hey guys," he called to the human tin soldiers. "Want a beer?" No one budged. He shrugged, grabbed a cold bottle out of the fridge, twisted the cap and slouched on the sofa.

When Miriam started to open her mouth, he leveled her with a look. "Don't start on me, okay? I've been a good boy and let you poke and push and correct until I'm about at my limit. I know how to talk and dress and act in public. My mother was a stickler on manners.''

Miriam smiled and sat beside him on the couch, her hands in her lap, her ankles crossed just so. He had an urge to tip her over, see what she'd do.

"What happened to that easygoing, laughter filled guy I met a month ago?"

"He misplaced his fiancée." Jace took a swig of beer, feeling the familiar twist in his gut. Aside from Devon's assurances that he was the best, Jace had hired his own men to search for Vickie. So far, no one had come up with anything.

Miriam placed a hand over his, gave a squeeze of compassion.

"I've been a jerk," he said, an apology. "I'm preoccupied."

"I understand."

"I shouldn't take it out on you, though. But this is all so crazy." He gestured around the condo where people were working away industriously. "I'm having trouble getting accustomed to all this royal stuff. I'm not used to people bowing and standing when I walk in a room. It's ridiculous and awkward."

"As CEO of your own business, don't your employees defer to you?"

"Defer?" He frowned. "They treat me with respect, as I do them. But they don't jump to attention or get all nervous when I come in the door. I operate my business as a team. The young man who runs my mail room is just as important as the vice president of marketing. And I treat him as such."

"It has obviously worked well for you. Your employees trust you and are loyal. Easton is like that to a point. He makes himself available to all those who seek attendance, will gladly accept a dinner invitation with someone of no rank—much to the frustration of the royal guardsmen."

"Then why all this fuss here?" Once again he gestured around his living room. "Why are you here trying to train me to be a stuffed shirt?"

"It is not my intent to turn you into a stuffed shirt. But there are ceremonies you must be prepared for, certain customs and rituals."

"Okay. But at home I can slouch on the sofa, agreed?"

She grinned. "As you are now?"

"Exactly." Now that they had that straight, he felt better. "So, does being the king's goddaughter give you special privileges?"

"Some." She smoothed her knee-length skirt, even though a wrinkle wouldn't dare mar it. "It helped me get this position."

"I doubt that. I think you got this position on your own merit. What do your folks do?"

"My father is the Lord of Funerals."

"Yikes. Depressing job."

"Oh, no. It is a very prestigious position. It predominately involves arranging banquets and such for families of the deceased. I would be next in line to succeed my father, but since I am a woman, it is not allowed."

"Huh?"

She shrugged.

"My assistant's a woman," he said, frowning. "She's the best party organizer in the state if you ask me. I'd trust her to handle my biggest account. And not just the party."

"You make the rules of your company."

"I don't get it. Easton doesn't hold to protocol naming an heir to the throne. He said himself he courted his granddaughters, so he obviously isn't biased against women."

"This custom involves a different branch of our government. It was originated by the king's great-grandfather, who my grandfather assisted."

"Would you take over your father's position if you could?"

"My father is a young man, so there are many years left in his service. But if he were unable to fulfill his duties, then yes, I would love to run it."

"Does Easton know how you feel?"

"No."

"You should tell him. He's the king. He can change the rules." As Jace would be able to if he accepted the appointment. He decided that would be one of the first things on his list. *If* he accepted.

The door opened and Devon walked in. Jace nearly spilled his beer coming to his feet. He met the other man halfway. "You found her."

Devon nodded, handed him a sheaf of papers. "She's in Seattle under an assumed name. Tory Coronado. She works at a hotel coffee shop."

Relief that she hadn't come to harm nearly buckled

his knees. The next emotion, though, was confusion. And hurt. She'd left on her own. Why?

Coronado. Interesting that she'd picked that name. He remembered her telling him that the hotel had been the reason she'd chosen California when she'd run away. If he were to be fanciful, he'd have to believe that the Hotel Del Coronado was what had ultimately brought them together.

Without another word to Devon, he went to his bedroom, tossing clothes into a suitcase, calling his pilot and arranging transportation to Seattle. He would rearrange the rest of his schedule on the way to the airport or on the jet.

When he turned around, Devon was blocking the doorway.

"Don't make me prove that I can go through you," he said.

Devon didn't budge. "I respect your need for privacy, but you're important to our country. The intended heir to the throne can't just go off unguarded. It'll be easier all around if you give in gracefully and let me accompany you." He gave an easy shrug. "You could try giving me the slip, but I've got all the information. I'd just follow."

Jace sighed in frustration. Time wasn't moving fast enough for him. They'd found Vickie. He wanted to be there. Now.

Although he found the idea of having a bodyguard ridiculous, Sir Devon Montcalm *was* turning out to be an asset.

"I'm leaving now. If you can keep up, have at it.

Otherwise, stay the hell out of my way. And thank you,'' he said belatedly.

Devon moved aside and let him pass, fell into step beside him. "You're welcome. And the day I can't keep up is the day Miriam's father arranges a party for my dead washed-up body.''

Jace grinned. That was as close to a joke as the solemn captain had come so far. Perhaps there was hope for the guy.

KRISSY KATWELL stretched like a sleek cat, shifting against the silk sheets of the bed. They'd been specially requested. She liked that.

Feeling restless, she tried to pick up the thread of conversation that had been interrupted by sex. It hadn't been great sex, but then again, she wasn't all that choosy.

"It's against my journalistic nature to sit on a story, you know. I've spent time and money on this—airfare to Oregon and Los Angeles. I've worked damned hard and it's a dynamite piece. The public will eat it up.''

He reached for his scotch on the bedside table, sat up and took a sip. Then he leaned back and stroked her perfumed skin. "How does your journalistic nature feel about being a queen?''

He'd rendered her speechless, and that rarely happened. She was forty-three, definitely considered an old maid. To go from never being married to a queen…

"Under those circumstances, I imagine I can exercise some patience.''

''That's my girl.''

''It's been a month, though. I can find a truckload of information on her past, but nobody can find where the little chit's gone off to. You really should have thought this out, made better arrangements. The idea was for her to run *to* him, rather than away. She should have acted like any other girl in love and gone straight into his protective arms, talked him out of the throne for the sake of their future.''

He felt his temper boil that she was questioning him. He took a gulp of scotch, gritted his teeth. He still needed her help. ''I know where she is.''

''You do?''

''Haven't I always told you to leave the smart details to me?''

''So what now?''

''Carradigne's on his way. Now we up the ante.''

Chapter Nine

Vickie had gotten so used to California's sunny weather, that the rain and gloom of Washington was taking a toll on her. Gray skies, constant drizzle and bad hair days. The sun was so confused it rarely peeped out before five in the afternoon. By that time, the moon was already gnashing at the bit to chase it away.

She could hardly drag herself through the day, had dropped a tray of pancakes and syrup this morning, and splashed a customer with hot coffee. Thank goodness only a few drops had landed on the man's sleeve.

She'd offered to pay the cleaning bill, but he'd eased her distress and told her no harm done.

Odd that she'd returned to Washington. She'd run from here so many years ago, vowed never to come back. Just went to show, she supposed, that it was human nature to cling to familiarity—no matter what kind of abrasive memories that familiarity evoked.

The café of the small, chain hotel was typically generic, except it did have a pretty courtyard seating area adjacent to the main dining room. Not many people made use of it. November in Seattle was cold.

She turned, and for the second time today, dropped a full tray of dishes.

Frozen, she couldn't even bend to pick up the scattered silverware and remnants of scrambled eggs that splattered the floor and her ankles.

Jace stood just inside the doorway, looking fit and tanned and...and for once, expressionless.

Her body trembled as he walked toward her. He never took his gaze off hers. The athletic grace of his movements was imbued with a subtle, dangerous determination, like a tawny lion staking a claim.

He stopped in front of her. "Tory, I presume?"

She couldn't meet his eyes. He put a finger under her chin, tipped it up, gently forcing her to look at him. "Why?"

The assistant manager of the café came out from the kitchen, glared. "Is there a problem here, Ms. Coronado?"

"No, sir. I'll have this cleaned up in a minute." Vickie stooped down, scraped eggs and jelly off the floor, shaking so hard her bones rattled.

Jace bent, handed her a fork, piled broken dishes on the tray. His fingers encircled her wrist, toyed with the bracelet he'd given her.

She froze. "You don't have to help," she whispered. "Please."

He stood when a busboy materialized and took over the cleaning. She could practically hear his thoughts. *Why did you return my ring and keep the bracelet?*

"We need to talk."

She shook her head. "I'm working."

"Take a break, Vickie, or we'll discuss this right here in front of everyone."

This wasn't the same easygoing Jace she knew and loved. This man was worried, and he was angry, and obviously not sure which emotion to let loose.

She saw Stan Lowell, the manager of the hotel, standing at the end of the dining counter, watching them.

"Wait here," she told Jace, and made her way over to Stan. She hated what she was about to do. But she saw no other choice.

"Stan, can I have five minutes?"

"Take the rest of the day. It's been a rough morning for you."

"I only need five minutes."

"I'm not docking your pay, Tory. Take the day."

"Thank you." Stan was a gentleman, and a gentle man. He'd hired her right away, and arranged for her to get a cut rate on a room at the hotel until she could find suitable living arrangements, confiding that she reminded him of his daughter. That had surprised her, because he looked too young to be the father of someone her age.

Then again, she knew something about having children when you were barely more than a child yourself.

She could feel Jace's gaze boring into her back. She thought she'd already experienced as much pain as one person could stand. She suddenly found she hadn't.

Her insides raw, nausea churning, she laid her hand

on Stan's lapel in what she knew would look like a loving caress.

Stan's expression barely changed. Unflappable, he was perfect to manage a hotel.

"I know this doesn't make sense, but I need your help. Please, would you just play along with me—if anyone asks, pretend that we're…together?"

He glanced over to where Jace was standing by the entrance to the café. "Are you in trouble?"

She shook her head.

"Are you afraid of that guy?"

"No." She sighed. "It's complicated."

"I need more than that, Tory, or I'll be tempted to call security."

"I don't need protection from Jace." Her throat ached with tears. She had to find her backbone or she'd blow everything. She twisted the rings on her finger. She'd made enough mistakes as it was.

"I'm in love with him. But for reasons I can't go into right now, I had to break our engagement."

"Looks to me like nobody gave him the message."

"Not in person. It was cowardly, but like I said, it's complicated. Will you help?"

He bent down and kissed her cheek, whispered, "I hope you know what you're doing. If you need me, you know where to find me."

"Thanks." She cleared her throat, took a breath and squared her shoulders. Removing her apron, she wiped her damp palms on her slacks and made her way toward Jace, walking past him until she reached the deserted lobby of the hotel.

Jace fell into step behind her. His blood was on low simmer at seeing the guy in the suit put his hands on Vickie, kiss her. Nothing was going as he planned. After weeks of panic and gut-wrenching worry, he should have swept her in his arms, kissed her as though the world was about to end, made sure she was unharmed and treated her like Dresden china.

But the minute he'd seen her, no chains binding her, no gun to her head, something inside him had snapped. He didn't normally fly off the handle before getting all the facts.

She turned to face him. Her eyes were sad, rimmed with fatigue. In San Diego, she'd worked long hours and attended school full-time, burning the candle at both ends, yet she'd never looked this wrung out and dejected.

"What the hell is going on?" *Smooth, Carradigne. Get a grip, would you?* He sighed. "I've been out of my mind with worry."

She licked her lips. "Didn't you get my note?"

"No."

"The ring?" Her voice raised in panic. "You didn't get it?"

"Yes. I got the ring." He frowned. "Are you referring to those two words as your *note?*"

She nodded. "I'm sorry."

"You're sorry? Are you telling me that out of the clear blue sky, you just decided to break up with me?" He shook his head. "I don't think so, Vickie. I know you better than that."

"Do you?" Her chin jutted out. "That's funny. I never knew *you* were a prince."

He raked a hand through his hair. "I suspected that had something to do with it. Listen, sweetheart. I haven't made up my mind. I wouldn't do that without talking it over with you first. If it bothers you—"

She cut him off, holding up a hand, coming within a breath of touching his chest, then pulling back. "I was making a point, Jace, that neither of us knows that much about the other." Her eyes darted away, focused on a potted palm filling the space between a grouping of deep cushioned chairs in the lobby.

"I used to live here in Seattle. I, uh, got a call after we left your parents' house—the next day actually."

The one that Devon had told him about, from the phone booth, he figured. Finally, they were getting somewhere.

She looked like a strong wind would blow her over, so he gestured to a sofa by the lobby fireplace. "Do you want to sit down?"

"No. This won't take long."

His gut tightened. That wasn't the tone he was expecting.

"Stan called. He—he's the manager here. We were...we were together before. When I lived here. He asked me to come back. I—I don't want to hurt you, Jace. I thought by returning the ring, you'd understand." She flicked her hair behind her ear. The sapphire hearts on her bracelet tinkled.

Jace put his hands in his pockets, carefully made his face blank, waited to see how much deeper she'd dig the hole. He didn't imagine Stan had flown to San Diego and scrambled the phone lines with a code designed in Korosol. And there hadn't been any calls from Seattle on her call list.

She still wouldn't look him in the eye. "I can't marry you Jace. I'm still in love with someone else."

She was a terrible liar. Still, true or not, the words pierced him like a stiletto buried to the hilt in his gut. Something was going on. Her chin was up and her shoulders square, but fear tightened the corners of her eyes.

He knew not to back her in a corner. Like a frightened animal, she'd bolt—as she'd done a month ago. He had to give her some space, and give himself some time to think, to find a way to break through her barriers.

"I'm sorry," she said quietly.

"Me, too. You could have trusted me, Vickie." Unwilling to push anymore, he turned and walked away.

VICKIE FELT like a limp dishrag that had been stomped on, ground in the dirt, then scorched over an open fire. The images could have been a page taken right out of her teenage years.

She'd been a throwaway kid. Lived on the dirty streets at times. Been burned by fire and by life.

She'd had a shot at changing all that, but the seeds of her beginnings had sprouted like devil grass, refusing to be choked out.

Oh, she would bounce back. She always did. When

the new school semester started here in Seattle, she would enroll again. That goal couldn't be snuffed.

Securing a career wouldn't smear anyone else's name, ruin anyone else's life. As long as she kept to herself.

If she hadn't broken her vow not to get involved with another man, none of this would be happening.... But then she would have missed out on something very special.

Although Stan watched her like a mother hen, she refused to take the day off that he'd offered. She needed to keep busy, needed to stay occupied so she wouldn't lose her mind and run after Jace, beg him to forget everything she'd said, to take her under his protective wing and slay her dragons.

No, she'd created these dragons on her own. And she'd live with them.

By rote, she poured coffee, cleared tables, pocketed tips and scribbled orders. Her lips felt frozen in a smile, her heart like a lead stone in her chest.

As she clipped an order ticket on the round, stainless-steel spinner for the chef, Stan called her name.

"Telephone's for you."

Her heart jumped in her throat. "Who is it?"

"A woman named Tiffany."

Oh, God. She missed Tiffany. Missed her life. She took the phone, smiled her thanks to Stan. "Tiff?"

Male laughter greeted her. More like a giggle. Adrenaline shot so fast, so hard, she had to grab the counter for support.

She should have realized Tiffany wouldn't have

known she was using the name Tory Coronado. How had this maniac caller known?

"Isn't it interesting how much one person can find out about another?" the voice said.

"What do you want?"

"Now is that any tone to take with a friend who's done you a favor?"

"I haven't asked for any favors."

"Then let's just say I'm a swell guy. Your friend Tiffany is a bit of a scatterbrain, but she's loyal. Even the best of pals can slip up, though. Which is how we found Darren Hawkins, of course. No love lost there," he said on a chuckle. "And not a drop of loyalty. I'd go so far as to say that fellow loathes you."

Vickie feared she was going to be sick. She didn't want to listen, couldn't hang up.

"Want to know your little girl's name?"

"No." The word slipped out in a harsh whisper.

"Andrea. Isn't that a pretty name? Shame you didn't have a hand in picking it. Did you have a different name in mind, Victoria?"

Her brain wanted to shut down. *Andrea.* Her throat ached and her heart squeezed. She felt Stan's hand on her arm, saw the concern on his face. Her own face was probably as pale as death.

"Seems to me a girl of fourteen ought to know where her roots come from."

"You leave her out of this!" Several customers in the diner looked around. She lowered her voice. "What do you want from me? I did what you asked. Why are you doing this?"

"I saw you talking to Carradigne."

Her gaze darted around the room. The hair on her neck stood up and her skin crawled. He was watching her. Oh, God. What had she gotten herself into?

"I didn't ask him to come here!"

He made a noncommittal sound in his throat. "Wasn't too hard for me to track down your Andrea. She still lives in Los Angeles, in case you wanted to know. Anyway, a few whispered words in Krissy Katwell's ears, and she'll let the Carradignes, your kid and the whole world in on your sordid mistakes."

"Please don't do this." Tears clogged her throat. Stan was about to grab the phone from her.

"Talk to your lover."

"He's—" The line went dead. *Not my lover anymore.*

The receiver slipped from her hand. Stan caught it, steadied her. "What the hell was that about?"

She shook her head. She didn't understand, didn't know if the sicko wanted her to talk to Jace or stay away from him. She only knew that she had to protect Andrea.

Andrea. Oh, God

"Tory? Talk to me."

"I don't want you involved. Anybody who gets close to me ends up in danger." She whipped off her apron. "I'm sorry, Stan. I've got to leave."

He stopped her with a hand on her arm, obviously realizing that leaving meant she didn't intend to come back. "Tell me how to help you."

"You can't. I have to go. Thank you for everything you've done for me."

"You still have a paycheck coming."

"Keep it to cover the cost of the room. I'll call you when I settle in somewhere, see if I still owe you any money." She kissed him on the cheek and hurried away, her gaze darting around the corners, her heart pounding as she rode the elevator to the eighth floor. Someone was watching her.

"Well, by damn," she said aloud to the unseen evil. "Watch me leave, then leave me and mine the hell alone! I won't sully your stupid kingdom if that's what you're worried about."

She felt like an idiot shouting at the control panel of the elevator. She wanted to sag against the wall, sleep for a week and hope this was all a bad dream when she woke. But it wasn't a dream.

Once again, she'd fallen in love with the wrong man. And now, she wasn't the only one who would pay the price.

An innocent girl, and a man with an important political future would suffer.

She wasn't going to let that happen.

JACE OPENED the hotel room door, surprised to find the manager standing in the hallway, looking grim.

Vickie's so-called lover.

He'd half expected it to be Devon. On the way to the airport, he'd managed to talk the captain into staying in San Diego. Neither of them had known what was behind Vickie's sudden flight, or the use of a telephone scrambling device, and if by chance it had something to do with the naming of an heir, Easton was as much a target as any of them. Especially since Devon still hadn't managed to decode that telephone number.

He imagined Devon had sent a replacement body-guard to Seattle. If he had, the guy was good, because Jace hadn't spotted him.

"Mr. Carradigne, my name is Stan Lowell—"

"So your name tag says." He was still a little peeved that this guy had kissed Vickie. Even if it was only on the cheek.

Stan glanced down at his jacket, then back up. "May I come in?"

Jace stepped back. He knew Stan Lowell wasn't her lover, knew there hadn't been any incoming calls from Seattle on her phone records. But Lowell's body radiated protective vibes like static on a windy day.

"I don't know what's going on, but I think Tory's in trouble. I'm not one to break a confidence, but I feel I owe it to you to tell you that she and I are not involved."

"I know."

Stan nodded. "Good. A few minutes ago, she got a phone call in the café. I took the call, and it was a woman's voice. She said her name was Tiffany."

"Tiffany's a friend of Vickie's from San Diego."

Stan frowned. "Vickie? You mean Tory?"

"Yes." Something stopped him from giving her real name just yet. He'd probably been hanging around Devon Montcalm too much.

"She went pale when she answered. I could hear a man's voice, not the woman who'd asked for her. It wasn't a pleasant conversation."

Jace went on alert. "What did Vickie say? Repeat the conversation for me."

Stan hesitated. "I'm going out on a limb here, trusting you on this."

"I'm in love with her, man. I've been out of my mind worrying if something had happened to her this past month. Tell me what you know so I'll know how to help her."

"I don't know much. It was an odd conversation, almost as though someone's blackmailing her. She said she hadn't asked for favors, told him to leave her alone, that she'd done what he asked. Then she said, 'I didn't ask him to come here.' I'm assuming she was talking about you, since you're the only one who has visited her."

"I was afraid of that." What the hell had they gotten into? "What else?"

"That's about it. She pleaded with him not to do something. She's terrified, but she wouldn't tell me why. She said anyone who gets close to her ends up in danger. She's packing to leave right now."

Jace bolted toward the door. He knew how quickly she could vanish without a trace. "Where is she?"

"Room 824."

"In this hotel?"

"Yes."

He snatched open the door. "Thanks, man. I owe you."

"Just take care of her," Stan called, but Jace was already down the hall, impatiently pounding on the elevator call button.

Instead of waiting, he raced to the stairwell, ran up the two flights to the eighth floor, made himself walk calmly down the hall toward room 824. She was scared. No sense scaring her even more. He needed control, finesse.

And if he got his hands on whoever was messing with Victoria, he was going to rip them limb from limb.

He knocked lightly on the door. He could hear her moving around inside, hear her freeze on the spot. Damn it.

"It's me, Vickie. Please open the door."

He waited. Patience had always been one of his strongest virtues. It was waning considerably. He was beginning to think he'd have to hunt up Stan and get a pass key when the door opened.

His heart nearly melted and broke at the same time. She'd been crying. Her blue eyes were filled with enough worry to topple a power pole. Beyond her, Sissy was sitting in the middle of an open suitcase half-filled with clothes.

"Jace, I told you, it's over between—"

"You lied." He stepped over the threshold, walked her back into the room, kicking the door closed behind him. Once again he found himself at odds. He'd intended to scoop her in his arms, pamper her, plead with her. His intentions got lost somewhere between the stairwell and the "Jace, I told you."

Part of him was annoyed that she hadn't trusted him. Another part of him was still slightly miffed over this other lover thing. The biggest part of him was in an all-out panic over the possibility of losing her.

He backed her up against the wall, pressed his knee between her legs, determined to show her that what they had was powerful, that a glitch in the road, no matter how huge, could be worked out.

"Let's just see how 'over' this is, hmm?" He lowered his mouth to hers, wasn't as gentle as he'd like to be. His belly was a cauldron of need and terror and love. All three were making him crazy. This woman was making him crazy. Damn it, she was his life.

Vickie flattened her hands against the wall behind her, stunned for a split second. Where always before Jace had been the soul of tenderness, now his touch was filled with demand.

A shot of fear zinged through her, thrilled her. Here was the powerful man who ran a Fortune 500 company, who commanded attention and made millions. A force to be reckoned with.

The hint of arrogance and danger radiated like a sensual yet snapping jolt of electricity. She melted into him, lifted her arms, wrapped them around his neck and clung. She kissed him with all the terror, love, hope and despair in her heart. She kissed him for the days they'd missed together, for the days they'd have to be apart.

She didn't realize she was crying, until a sob broke. "Oh, God. Vickie. Sweetheart." He lifted her, cradled her, sat with her in the chair and held her. "Shh. I'm sorry. Damn it. Did I hurt you? Scare you?"

"No." She said it into his shirtfront. She wished she could stay right here, just like this, for the rest of her life.

He stroked her hair. "Tell me what's going on."

Fresh tears welled. She knew she had to level with him, but she hated the disillusion she'd surely see in his eyes. But it was better all around if he heard it from her, rather than reading about it in the paper.

She tried to scoot off his lap. He held her back.

"I need to get up," she said.

"Every time I let you go, I lose you."

She satisfied herself by stroking his handsome face, the dimple in his cheek that remained even when he wasn't smiling. Lines fanned from the sides of his eyes, his mouth. Character lines.

He was a man of great character.

"I'm not going far." She slid off his lap, took a breath, let it out. "I should never have accepted your proposal without first telling you about my past."

"I told you that doesn't matter."

"Obviously it does to someone. Because they're threatening to make it public. And I can't let that happen. I *won't* let it happen."

"Vickie—"

"You're not going to put me off again, Jace. You might as well know what the whole world's likely to find out, so just hush up and listen."

Chapter Ten

"Did you see the write-up in the paper last month in Krissy Katwell's syndicated column?"

"Nobody pays attention to that gossip stuff, Vickie."

"Spoken like a man with nothing to hide." She paced to the other side of the room, glanced back when she heard him shift. "Stay over there, okay? I'm about to knock myself off this pedestal you've put me on, and I'd just as soon not see the disillusionment in your eyes while I'm doing it."

"You know, you're starting to piss me off."

"Ditto."

"Ditto? What the hell have you got to be mad about? I'm the one who got left without a word."

His tone of voice shoved her right to the edge. "You think everything's so hunky-dory and positive and will come out smelling like roses. Well, baby, let me tell you, I've got a whole lot of pissed-off years bottled up inside me, years I've tried to forget, to suppress." She moved Sissy off the bed, slammed her suitcase shut. The cat shot under the table and hid near her travel cage.

"I turned over a new leaf, butter wouldn't melt in my mouth. I didn't sleep around, didn't break any laws, paid my bills on time, helped out other people in need, busted my butt to be Suzy Citizen."

She faced him now, hands on hips, all the emotions of the past four weeks boiling to the surface. "I fall in love with you, start believing the stupid fairy tale—do you know I even looked on the Internet to see if anyone made glass slippers?" She nearly shouted it, didn't give him time to respond.

"I haven't indulged in fairy tales since I was a kid. So I'm an idiot. And then I get these phone calls telling me I'm not princess material. Well, duh. I had a baby when I was sixteen. The boy who got me pregnant didn't stick around. I did something good and decent and gave that little girl up for adoption so *she* could have the fairy tale, the perfect family.

"Then I shacked up with an ex-con who hadn't quite learned the meaning of the word reform. He sold drugs out of our apartment, and I nearly went to jail as an accessory. I've slept on the streets, in cardboard boxes, in the backs of cars—and not always alone."

Her heart was pounding in her chest, her palms sweating. "I'm shamed right down to my toes, but I can't change any of it. I thought I could outrun it, be better, put it behind me. I was wrong, damn it. Again."

She hadn't realized he'd gotten up. Her vision had

glazed, her mind turned inward. When he put his arms around her she jerked, tried to shrink back.

"Stop it. Come on, sweetheart." He pulled her close, held her. "Shh. It'll be okay."

She wadded his shirt in her fist, brought it down against his chest. "Would you stop saying that."

He lifted her right into his arms as though she were a child, sat with her in the chair, held her in his lap once more.

"I'm not letting you go, Vickie, so you might as well relax and stop fighting me. I know that's what you expect, what life has conditioned you for. But this is a new slate. Just like you said. And I don't fold when the going gets rough. I love you."

She'd been strong all her life. It had taken strength to survive on her own. She'd made mistakes, yes, but she'd always led with her chin, rarely let tears betray her.

With Jace, she couldn't seem to muster that control.

Tears slipped silently down her cheeks. He pressed her face against his neck, stroked her hair, her back.

"Oh, man. Come on, sweetheart. Please don't do that."

The sheer masculine helplessness in his voice brought a watery chuckle. She lifted the hem of her shirt, used it to swipe at her face. She hated to cry. It made her nose red and her head ache and it was weak. She had no use for weaklings.

"I don't get it. Do you have a psycho ex or something? Why are people threatening me?"

"No ex. Psycho or otherwise." Still stroking her hair, he said quietly, "Tell me about the phone calls."

"Sunday morning, after we'd been to your parents' house, I got up and saw the article in the paper." She plucked at a snag on her flannel shirt. "I've checked every day here in Seattle, but Krissy hasn't written any more about either of us. I've even bought all the gossip magazines. The guy at the newsstand must think I don't have a life."

He continued to stroke her hair. "The phone calls?" he reminded.

"I'm getting there." She shifted in his lap, knowing she shouldn't be allowing him to hold her this way, unable to gather the energy to do anything about it. His palm was gentle against her hair, his other hand warm against her hip.

"It was pretty much like I said. He knows about Darren—the guy in prison," she clarified. "He threatened to feed this Katwell woman more information for her column if I didn't leave town, said my reputation would ruin your chances to be a king."

"That's a crock."

"No, it's not, Jace. I knew I should have told you about my past, but every time I tried, you shushed me." Her cheek lay against his chest and she was glad she wasn't looking at him. "I'm ashamed of some of the things I've done."

"You have nothing to be ashamed of."

"Easy for you to say." She'd been conditioned to react that way. "Anyway, I realized if they knew about Darren and wanted to dig deeper into my life history, they'd probably contact him. I was nineteen when I was with Darren. Young and still stupid. He was older and I'd convinced myself I was in love. I told him about the baby.''

''And you think he'll pass on that information?''

''I know he will. I testified against him in a drug trial, helped put him in prison. If a person's looking to dig up secrets, an illegitimate child is too good to pass up. I was terrified someone would try to track down my daughter, mess up her life, as well as yours. So, I packed up Sissy and left.'' She felt the muscles in his arms bunch.

''And the next call?''

''It was several hours after you got here, today. He knew you were here, like he was watching us. He said he found my daughter, that her name's Andrea and she's in Los Angeles.''

Jace swore. ''Could that be true?''

''She was born close to L.A.''

''This doesn't make a lot of sense. Why are they harassing you?''

''They don't want me to ruin your chance at being king. Aren't you listening? He said your reputation is impeccable—and mine's not.''

He gently patted her hip, soothed her. ''It still doesn't jibe. You left town. That should have been the end of it. Why go to the trouble to search for your daughter, involve her? I'm fairly new to this game of royal politics, but it sounds to me like someone doesn't want me to accept this position. Maybe they can't find a way to discredit me, so they're going through you to get at me. Maybe they were banking on you being so scared you'd talk me out of accepting the crown.''

''That's a lot of maybes.''

''I'm thinking aloud here.''

Outside the window, the moon had won out after all, and the sky had turned dark. Rain pelted the windowpanes like gritty sheets of sand.

Vickie wondered if she should draw the drapes. This eerie feeling of being watched was giving her the creeps. They were on the eighth floor of the hotel, had an unobstructed view of Seattle's Space Needle. She doubted anyone could see in unless they were hanging from a window washer's scaffolding.

''When was your daughter born?'' he asked softly.

''September tenth. Two days before my seventeenth birthday at the county hospital in San Bernardino.'' With her thumb, she idly traced the gold of her sapphire rings. ''She turned fourteen this past September.''

''And the baby's father?''

''He'd left long before Andrea was born.'' She probably shouldn't be addressing the child by a name. She wasn't even sure the information was correct—or just a bluff. And a name made it so much more real, so much more heartbreaking.

''You must have been scared.''

''Yes. But there was a nurse—Hilary Fennes. She was kind to me.''

''I'm glad you had someone with you,'' he whispered.

They were silent for a while, and Vickie felt herself drifting. She was so tired, so overwhelmed. But she was afraid to sleep.

"How come you never mentioned you were a prince?"

"Being ninth in line is like claiming you're a full-blooded Native American because your great-grandmother was married to a man who was one quarter Cherokee. I've known about my ancestors, but it wasn't part of my lifestyle. Nor did I ever dream it would become one."

"The king's sister was your grandmother?"

"Yes. Her name was Magdalene, Easton's only sister. She was ten years younger than him. Her father had arranged for her to marry a wealthy English duke, but she was in love with another man. When her father got wind of the affair, he put a stop to it. Her lover was the captain of the royal guard, and King Cyrus didn't consider him good enough, so he transferred the guy to active duty where he was killed in a *peaceful* siege in Asia."

"That's awful." The room was quiet, with only the soft tap of the rain against the windows, an occasional howl of the wind. A single lamp burned, lending a cozy air to the room. With Jace's arms around her, it was hard to remember that safety—even emotional safety—was a tenuous thing.

"In those days things were different. Magdalene was pregnant with my dad when she found out the news, and she refused to marry the duke, even when her father threatened to disown her. He shipped her off to a convent until my dad was born. She developed a fever and died two days later.''

"Oh, my gosh. What happened to your dad?"

"Easton wanted to take him and raise him along with his three sons, but the king wouldn't hear of it. He didn't want the Carradigne name disgraced. The public didn't know that Magdalene was pregnant when she left society—everyone believed that she and the duke had just had a change of heart and decided they didn't suit, and that she'd gone off for some privacy.''

"The people still loved her.'' She nearly sighed.

"Very much. So King Cyrus gave my dad to his cousin here in California, Sir Walter Carradigne and his wife, Judith—my grandparents. At least the one's I've always known as my grandparents. They'd never had a child of their own and they were thrilled to get the baby.''

"Did your dad know he was adopted?"

"Yes, though no one's ever known the name of his father until Easton told us a couple of weeks ago. Dad's always been aware he has the legal right to the title of prince, but he's never used it, didn't pass it on to Kelly and me.''

"Did your dad ever go back to Korosol? If he didn't know his father's name did he wonder about his roots?'' Did her own daughter wonder about hers?

Jace gently kissed the top of her head. "He's never told me whether or not that was important to him. Easton has kept in touch with my dad over the years, though, and after King Cyrus passed on, Dad visited Korosol a few times.''

"That's a tragic story. I'm glad it had a happy ending."

He chuckled. "You and your fairy tales." He reached in his pocket, drew out the engagement ring and held it in his open palm in front of her. "While we're on the subject of happy endings, will you put this back on?"

She closed her eyes, told herself she was not going to cry anymore for the next century. It felt as though a thousand stinging wasps had been turned loose in her stomach as she gently closed his fingers around the ring, squeezed and let go.

"Vickie?"

She scooted off his lap. "I can't, Jace."

"I've just told you there's scandal in my family tree. That makes us even. Whatever we have to face, we can face it together. Nothing's too big that it's going to topple a country."

The parallel she knew he was attempting to draw fell short. "Today's media is a different breed. You know that. They'll dissect your life to death—and mine. Somebody will want to do a book, you can be sure, and they'll dig and research. It'll not only hurt you—"

"Let me handle me, Vickie."

"That's fine. But as I was going to say, you're not the only one involved. My daughter and her family are now part of this, too. I have no way of knowing if she even knows she's adopted. What if they've decided not to tell her? Think of how that could devastate her. She didn't ask for any of this. And whoever is making these calls...how do we know he won't follow through, or that he doesn't have something more dangerous in mind?'' She shook her head, looked at him with all the agony that filled her heart and soul.

''You and me together are putting her at risk. I have to protect Andrea, make sure her world stays safe.'' Just saying her daughter's name made her heart jump in her throat.

''Don't start putting up roadblocks. I'm a wealthy man. We'll find her ourselves. Surround her with bodyguards.''

''We can't!'' Her stomach twisted into even tighter knots. ''How do we explain why that's necessary without upsetting her entire way of life?''

''Tell her parents. Let them decide.''

''If I just stay away from you, she'll be safe. There'll be no need for all this.''

''Can you be so sure? Whoever's behind these threats is nuts. Someone obviously doesn't want me to uphold my birthright and title in Korosol. They should be aiming their efforts at me, yet they're picking on you because you're more vulnerable. That's the M.O. of a coward. And that kind of person is a wild card.''

''Exactly, damn it! We don't know *what* they'll do! I should have followed my instinct and never gotten involved with you.'' The instant she said the words she regretted them, didn't mean them, wanted to take them back. The hurt on his face cut her to the quick.

''Jace...'' She reached out, clutched his arm. The muscles beneath his sweater were coiled and rock-hard. "I didn't mean it. I'm just so scared," she whispered.

He drew her to him, rested his head on the top of hers. "I know. I hate that I've put you in this position."

"You didn't mean to." Even so, they were in a mess.

Who they were together would never work.

Someone would always be taking shots at them, figuratively and perhaps literally. It wasn't just the two of them at stake. If that were the case, Vickie might have had fewer qualms, might've taken a chance on braving the scandalous storm.

But it wasn't just the two of them.

Her Cinderella fantasy did a final crash and burn. The nasty stepmother had turned up—and she didn't even know his name.

She'd have to accept it.

But she also had to accept that Jace had a valid point. He had funds and connections at his disposal that she didn't. On her own, the chances of protecting the daughter she'd never met were slim. Someone else had a head start on her. She didn't have the resources needed to defuse this time bomb.

Jace *did* have those resources. With him, she had a better chance of finding the adoptive parents, warning them, letting Jace protect them.

"Do you think we can find her?" she asked quietly into his sweater.

Jace tightened his hand around the ring, the diamond cutting into his palm. He could feel the weariness in Vickie's bones, wondered that she was even standing after all she'd been through. Not just the past four weeks, but over the course of her life.

She might consider her past an embarrassment. He considered it amazing. She was amazing. He wasn't sure he'd have fared as well without the loving support of his family.

"We'll find her. I'll make some calls and we'll head out in the morning. I came in the company jet. We can be in Los Angeles in a matter of hours."

"Shouldn't we leave now?"

"There's nothing we can do tonight. I'll set the wheels in motion and we can get started a little before dawn, be there by the time the city opens for business."

He set her away from him, stroked the hair back from her face. "Do you have a nightgown in that suitcase?"

Her eyes flared with a yearning that made him go from zip to hard in an instant.

"Yes...I have several."

"Why don't you find it and I'll run you a bath."

She stared at him for several seconds. Then she lifted her chin. "I think I can manage to turn a couple of knobs."

He almost smiled. He knew she'd been expecting him to suggest lovemaking, not a solitary bath. Hell, he'd give up a vital body part to do just that. But she'd been through enough, fought alone for so long.

He kissed her forehead, stepped around her. "Let me take care of you tonight."

STEAM FILLED the bathroom when he turned and saw her standing in the doorway, a cotton nightshirt clutched in her hand. He'd poured a generous amount of bath gel under the running water, and the tub filled with fragrant bubbles.

"Were you going to stay and watch?" she asked. "Or...join me?"

"Do you want me to?"

She looked away, as though suddenly shy. He stepped toward her, took the gown from her hand, eased the flannel shirt off her shoulders. "Next time, okay?"

He saw her eyes turn liquid, knew she was thinking there wouldn't be a next time. He wanted to shake her, *make* her believe in him. Instead, he kissed her eyelids, let himself out the bathroom door and closed it behind him.

Sissy had finally slunk from beneath the table. He scooped the cat up, scratched her ears. "You've been a good pal, haven't you?" The cat purred for a moment, then wiggled to get down, making herself comfortable in the middle of the pillows.

Vickie's room key was on the dresser. He pocketed it and quietly went out the door. He didn't intend to leave her alone tonight, and there was no sense keeping a room in his name for all and sundry to get wind of.

A burly guy dressed in a black suit sat by the ice machine pretending to read a newspaper. One of Devon's men. He wondered if this was the one with the driving skills of an ant. Probably not. Devon didn't strike him as a man who'd take too lightly to one of his trained men getting one-upped. This guy had managed to stay hidden all day. Now he was sitting in plain view. A dare to anyone who cared to breach his territory.

Good. Nobody would be get getting past the elevator or stairwell tonight who didn't belong.

He was ninety-nine percent sure this was Devon's replacement, but he wouldn't gamble that one percent. Pausing on his way to the stairs, he rapped his knuckles on the newspaper. "Call your boss."

The guy took out a cell phone, punched a button and handed the phone to Jace, at the same time reaching into the inside pocket of his jacket.

"What's your man's name," Jace said the minute the line clicked.

"Keegan Burnaby." Even as Devon said the name, Keegan was holding up his identification. "Thanks, I'll get back to you."

He returned the phone to Burnaby. "No hard feelings."

"None taken."

"I'll be back in five minutes. Ten tops."

Keegan nodded.

As soon as he got to his room, he flipped on his cell phone, called down to the front desk and asked for Stan.

When the other man came on the line, he said, "Can you check me out?"

"Are you leaving?"

"In the morning. But as far as anyone else is concerned, I'm not here."

"There was an inquiry. She said she was your sister, Kelly. I told her you weren't registered. I hope that was all right."

"Perfect." Kelly would have called his cell phone if she needed him. "Thanks, Stan. For everything."

"Is Tory okay?"

"She will be. We'll be in touch." As soon as he disconnected, he punched in Devon Montcalm's private number.

"Glad to know you're using your head and not trusting anyone," the captain said.

"I still don't like this bodyguard stuff. Makes me nervous when I don't know the good guys from the bad ones. The phone call to Vickie from San Diego was a threat," he said as he zipped his duffel bag. He hadn't unpacked yet.

"She got another call right after I arrived in Seattle. Did you get a line on that phone number yet?"

"I traced it back to one of the king's valets. He's claiming one of my men had access to his phone. I've placed them both in custody and sent them back to Korosol. Still don't know who jammed my computer. It has to be someone in Korosol."

"How do you take someone in custody for making a phone call?"

There was another one of those silences Devon was so fond of. That dim bulb thing.

"Tell me what you know," Devon said.

"There are some incidents in Vickie's past..." He was reluctant to discuss her private business, but knew there was no other recourse.

"I'm aware of the details," Devon said.

Jace sighed. He should have figured the guy would do a thorough check. "How long?"

"Since you announced the engagement. It's standard procedure."

"It's invasion of privacy," he snapped. He was tired. It was a stupid accusation. Someone else was invading her privacy in a big way—and threatening to make it public. "Sorry. Why didn't you say anything?"

"Figured it was Vickie's business to tell or not."

That one statement cemented Jace's trust in the other man. Integrity and loyalty were two indisputable qualities in a man. Devon possessed them in spades.

"Too bad this Katwell woman doesn't share your ethics."

"I've had dealings with her in the past. It's not easy to shut her up. Frankly, I'm surprised she hasn't already jumped the gun. My guess is, someone's making it worth her while to stall."

Jace brought him up to date on the latest phone call, and discussed his theory that someone didn't want him to accept the king's appointment.

"I'd already come to that conclusion," Devon said.

"Nice of you to let me in on it." He rubbed the back of his neck where it was knotted with stress. "What if I just let it be known that I'm declining Easton's offer?"

"You're still part of the royal family. It won't stop

Katwell from printing what she knows. Even if you break it off with Vickie, she'll still be the ex-fiancée of a prince. That makes her fodder for the gossip rags.''

By association, he'd landed Vickie in a no-win situation. Whether he upheld his duty or not, the private details of her life were already gathering in someone's folder, waiting to be exposed.

''Vickie and I are taking the jet to L.A. in the morning. We need to find the adoptive family, run some interference.''

''I understand where you're coming from, Jace, but it's risky. I can't guarantee that the two men I've taken into custody has plugged the leak. From what I can tell, they've been relying on us to do the legwork, then making their move. Besides, the adoption records are sealed. I've checked. If Vickie knows something personally, you could be leading the wrong people right to the girl.''

''I think we still have to chance it. Even if it's a bluff, the family has to be warned.'' He raked a hand through his hair, glanced at the heavy drapes covering the hotel room window. ''Is it impossible to get a line on this adoption information?''

''Nothing's impossible.''

''Then we have to try. If Katwell's digging, she'll have some powerful resources.''

''I'd like to think ours are stronger.''

''Let's hope so. The baby was born fourteen years ago at a county hospital in San Bernardino, California. September tenth. There's a nurse I'd like to get in touch with—Hilary Fennes. That's as much as I know for now. The caller claims the girl lives somewhere in L.A., and that her first name is Andrea. See what you can find out on your end. I'll call you in the morning from the air and let you know our arrival time."

He hung up the phone, grabbed his bag and jogged back down the hall and stairs.

Using the key he'd taken, he let himself into the room. Vickie gasped and froze in the middle of the room. The bathroom door was open, letting out a flow of steam and scent. Her nightshirt hung to her knees, had very little shape, but it still managed to outline every one of her curves.

His body tightened, and he mentally recited the names of the cabinet members in the Korosolan government he'd so carefully memorized at Miriam Kerr's behest.

Closing the door behind him, he said. "Sorry. I thought I'd get back before you were out. I didn't mean to scare you."

She shrugged. "I'm jumpy. I thought you'd left." She glanced at the duffel bag he set on the chair.

"I checked out of my room. Stan's already making sure no one knows I'm at the hotel. He's a decent guy."

"Yes." She still hadn't moved from the spot midway between the bathroom and the bed.

He scooted Sissy off the pillows and turned back the heavy spread. "Come on. You look like a strong wind will blow you over."

"Thanks so much for the compliment." She

climbed under the covers, glanced up at him. "Where are you sleeping?"

He sat on the side of the mattress. "With you."

"Oh."

He stroked her hair, hated the circles of fatigue and worry beneath her eyes. "Not that kind of 'oh.' When I make love with you again, I'd like for us both to be a little more into it."

"Jace—"

"Shh," he whispered. "Go to sleep. I'll watch over you." He knew she'd been going to tell him they wouldn't be making love anymore—despite her actions to the contrary just before her bath, when he'd seen that brief flash of vulnerability and desire. She wouldn't accept the engagement ring, was certain they couldn't be together. He had to convince her otherwise.

Her eyes started to close, then popped open. "What about Sissy?"

"I'll take care of it. She can fly with us to Los Angeles. We'll rent a car at the airport and my pilot can take Sissy to San Diego. I'll get Kelly to pick her up."

Vickie would have laughed at the eccentricity of a cat being flown around in a private jet, but she flat-out didn't have the energy.

It was just as well that Jace didn't have sex in mind, because she simply didn't think she was up to the task. The way she felt right now, she'd have an orgasm and probably keel over from a heart attack.

The ridiculous thought had her wondering if she

was on the verge of hysteria. It was the idea that someone was watching her every move, she decided.

"You really shouldn't be here," she said.

"I have a feeling this is exactly where someone
wants me to be. I talked to Devon. He agrees. This all
started when Easton arrived. Somebody out there
wants me to change my mind. It's a pity, because I
haven't accepted in the first place."

"You have to, Jace. It's your right and your duty."

And that duty was sitting very heavily on his shoulders. "You have a say in it, too."

She shook her head, started to speak. He pressed his
finger over her lips, but she reached up and removed
his hand, held it for a moment.

"What if we can't find the adoptive parents?"

"You don't know Sir Devon Montcalm very well
to ask a question like that." He smiled. "We'll find
them. Let them decide what they want to do. Then
we'll move heaven and earth to make that happen."

"I hate this."

"I know." He stroked her hair, her temples, her
eyelids, urging them to close.

"I'm glad you're here."

"Me, too. Sleep now."

Chapter Eleven

Vickie gazed out the window of the Learjet, and stroked her hand over Sissy's fur. Since they weren't on a commercial flight, Sissy didn't have to stay in her pet carrier.

The cat wasn't too sure about the trip. She'd just now come out of hiding in the bathroom, leapt up into the seat next to Vickie and stared out of eyes filled with accusation.

"I know moving around has been difficult, but really, Sissy, you ought to be strutting like a peacock. What other cat do you know who gets first-class treatment like this? You could be riding in the cargo hold or the back seat of my car."

Sissy stretched and gave her a bored look, her ears twitching. "Okay, a peacock was a poor analogy since it's in the bird family. How about a female lion?"

The cat relented and snuggled close.

"That's better," she whispered, not wanting to disturb Jace while he was on the phone. He'd already arranged for someone to pick up her car and take it back to San Diego.

Regardless of the outcome of their relationship, she'd be glad to get back to California. That's where her job and school and apartment were—provided the apartment was still available.

She knew her job was waiting. She'd called to let Tiffany and Paul know that she was okay. Even though she'd left for a good reason, sacrificed her entire way of life for Jace, she felt awful at causing so many people worry.

When Jace had called his mother, Annie Carradigne had insisted on talking to Vickie. She didn't ask for details, simply let Vickie know that she was family and family stuck together.

The genuine caring had made her weep, even though she'd told herself she was finished with tears.

Jace was still pacing the aisles of the luxurious jet, cell phone clipped to his belt, an earplug and miniature microphone allowing him to make call after call hands free.

The apparatus was so tiny it looked like the latest invention for a Ken doll.

She had no idea who he was talking to now. Some of his calls had to do with business. Most of them had to do with her. She'd been shamelessly eavesdropping.

He hadn't been exaggerating when he'd said he had contacts. He had people jumping through hoops with little more than a soft command. Just watching him in action gave her a fluttery feeling inside. He was a powerful man.

An incredibly special man.

On her own, she doubted she'd have known where to start in this search for her adopted daughter. Nerves crowded in her belly, a thousand "what ifs" racing through her mind.

Vickie wondered if her own mother had lived, would she have tried to reconnect those ties? Probably. Having someone was better than being absolutely alone.

But her own daughter wasn't alone. She'd made sure of it.

Did she wonder, though? Did she even know she was adopted? Did she understand it had been a loving sacrifice, or did she feel hatred, believe her birth mother had thrown her away like last night's garbage?

Oh, God, the wondering was making her a wreck. She shouldn't be delving into these mental questions. She'd done the right thing, the unselfish thing. She'd given her baby to a family who'd raise her with love, shower her with dolls on her birthday, buy her pretty ribbons for her hair, take her to ballet lessons and Girl Scouts and kiss her tears away when her first case of puppy love broke her heart. They would buy her the cutest prom dress, watch her cheer at the high school football games, weep when she went off to college and dance with her at her wedding.

A sixteen-year-old, with no home or family could never have provided those things. Once Vickie had discovered she was pregnant, there were no perfect choices left. She'd made the best decision she could.

She looked up when Jace finally disconnected the

phone, removed his headset and sat down beside her, reaching over to stroke Sissy's fur. The cat purred. She knew a good thing when she felt it.

"Got all your ducks in a row?" She needed to banish these nerves. They had a difficult journey ahead of them.

"Most of mine. Some of yours. An accident up north downed one of our cell sites. Had some customers hit a flat spot with no service and get a little antsy."

"Did you get it fixed?"

"Yeah. I've got a great team behind me. And I'm not worried. Our service covers more area than our competitors. Business is solid. Which reminds me. I'm getting you a cell phone. I don't want to ever go through what I did before, not being able to get in touch with you."

"That was the idea," she reminded him quietly.

He glanced at her. "And I'm still annoyed about it." His grin belied that annoyance. "Anyway, I could have at least left pleading messages for you. I'd have worn you down."

"You're so sure of yourself."

"That's the only way to be."

His heel was tapping on the floor as though he had an excess of energy and didn't know what to do with it. She put her hand on his knee. "You'll shake the plane out of the sky."

He laughed, covered her hand, raised a brow when she tried to remove it. Rather than wrestle, she left it there. A minute later his knee was bouncing again. Energy or nerves? she wondered.

"Did you call my landlord?"

The shaking stopped. "No."

"Jace. We talked about this. What if he rents my apartment?"

"Then you can move in with me. You'll be living there anyway. If you don't like it, we'll build a house. Wherever you want. Whatever you want."

She pulled her hand from beneath his. "Don't start, okay? I've already told you there are too many ifs to think about the future."

"I can feel my annoyance climbing again."

He made her crazy. And he made her want to laugh. "Tough. Can I use your phone?"

He sighed. "The manager's holding your apartment, Vickie. I paid the rent through the end of the year. That doesn't mean I won't try to talk you out of using it."

"Let's just get through one thing at a time, okay?"

He picked up her hand, linked his fingers with hers. "I'm a multitask kind of guy. But I'll give it a try."

WHEN THEY LANDED the private jet at LAX, Devon was already there to meet them, a rental car standing by.

Vickie put an annoyed Sissy into her pet carrier, kissed her goodbye and followed Jace off the plane.

Sir Devon Montcalm leaned against a post inside the arrival gate, appearing relaxed, yet she imagined he knew the color of eyes, hair and dress of everyone around him within fifty yards. He wasn't a man for small talk, and from the way he carried himself, a person would be a fool to cross him.

"Good to see you again, Ms. Meadland."

"Please, call me Vickie." She felt a wash of embarrassment that Devon Montcalm had spent so much time tracking her down.

He nodded. "Need help with the bags?"

They'd left most of her belongings on the plane—including her cat—to be flown to San Diego.

"We've just got two bags," Jace said, following Devon through the terminal. They didn't speak until they'd reached the full-size sedan and secured the luggage in the trunk.

"Did you find out anything?" Jace asked.

Devon glanced at Vickie. She had an idea he was waiting for her to get in the car. "You might as well tell us both," she said, standing her ground. "Otherwise, Jace will just have to repeat himself."

Devon withdrew a piece of paper. "The nurse is retired and lives in Riverside. That's her home address. It'll take me another day or two to trace the adoption records. Perhaps this woman will be a shortcut."

Jace took the paper from Devon and handed it to Vickie. Her fingers shook as she accepted it. One step closer. She thought she might hyperventilate.

Jace noticed, of course. He didn't miss much.

"You okay?"

She took a breath, let it out. "Yes. Peachy." *You will not throw up,* she told herself. *Or faint, or scream, or stick your head in the nearest toilet.* She was certain Jace could cite one of his famous Carradigne rules covering all of those behaviors. Good grief, she was losing it.

He turned back to Devon, reluctantly, it seemed. The other man was also watching her as though she was going to combust before his very eyes.

"Anything on the caller?" Jace asked.

"Yes. My plane's standing by. As soon as I brief Burnaby and get you going, I'm headed for New York."

"About Burnaby. He's good. I've got nothing against the man, but I don't like the idea of having a tail. Like I told you, this is touchy enough without stumbling over someone else."

"I'm not negotiating on that. King's orders. As it was, I had to talk His Majesty out of sending the entire Royal Guard."

Before Jace could ask why, Devon handed him a gun wrapped in a manila folder. "Just in case. It's a forty-five automatic. I'm told you're familiar with fire-arms."

"That's not going to appease the cop who pulls me over and catches me carrying concealed."

Devon handed over another envelope. "These are papers on the gun, a permit to carry."

Jace raised a brow, said dryly, "You think of everything, don't you? I happen to know that process takes a while, has certain requirements."

Devon just stared back at him, nodded at the envelope. "That's all the requirement you need."

He didn't question further. He knew money could cut through red tape. And so could political connections.

"So, are you going to tell me why you're going to New York, and why you think I might need this gun?"

"The king's grandson, Markus Carradigne."

Jace frowned. Grandson? He hadn't heard about this one. "I thought Kelly and I were Easton's last hope for heirs."

"You are. Easton will do anything in his power to make sure Markus doesn't take over the throne."

"And this Markus. He wants it?"

"Yes. He wants it. His father, Byron, should have been the next in line, but while he and his wife were on vacation in Africa, their jeep exploded. We don't have solid enough proof to act on, but I'd stake my rank on Markus's involvement in his parents' deaths."

Jace swore, more than a little peeved that no one had bothered to tell him this, and there had been plenty of opportunities.

It dawned on him that Easton had only spoken about seven of the heirs. Three granddaughters in New York, and four grandsons in Wyoming. He'd been so stunned by Easton's arrival and all the information dropped on him at once, he hadn't done the math.

Markus would be first in line. After his father, that is. And his father was dead—under suspicious circumstances. Now Jace had a gun in his jacket and a license to carry it.

Hell. He thrived on excitement, but this was more

than he'd bargained for. Especially because it involved Vickie.

More than ever, Jace felt the weight of responsibility and duty on his shoulders.

For the past month, Easton had brought the country of Korosol alive for him. He felt a part of it already, had a stake in what happened.

Now, he understood Easton's desperation. The man was dying, and his beloved country stood to fall into unstable hands.

"Why wasn't I told about this?"

"You were guarded."

"Vickie wasn't!"

Devon had the grace to look away. "My first tip was Krissy Katwell's column. She pulled some stunts in New York with the princesses. We found out she was getting her information from Winston Rademacher, Markus's advisor."

"So, where's this Rademacher character?"

"Dead."

What the hell had he stepped into the middle of? "And you think someone's taken his place?"

"Maybe. That's what I hope to find out in New York. Because of who he is, it's not that easy to keep Markus under surveillance. He's a chameleon—a spoiled little boy in private, a charmer in public. There are people in our country who believe he should rightfully succeed Easton on the throne. Some of his supporters have powerful connections, we know that. But we don't know *all* of his followers."

"Some of them could be in Easton's cabinet?"

Devon nodded. "It would explain the leaks. Why he's continually one step ahead of us. I don't believe the two men I already have in custody are the only ones involved."

"*If* it's Markus," Jace reminded him. He looked over at Vickie to see how she was taking this news. Her blue eyes dominated her face, but her mouth was set in a firm line. She looked as if she'd dearly love to have five minutes alone in a room with this Markus Carradigne.

He nearly smiled. She might appear delicate, but she was a survivor. She'd fight for those she loved. He knew that for certain because she'd left everything she loved to protect him.

He felt the weight of the gun in his hand. From now on, Vickie wasn't going to have to worry about protection. He would take care of her—and anyone close to her.

He opened the car door for her, then slid the gun in the glove compartment.

"Burnaby's watching your back," Devon said. "But you watch it, too. I don't want to be scraping your carcass off somebody's carpet."

"Morbid, aren't you?" He smiled slightly. "I can take care of myself."

"Yeah, well see that you do."

"And tell Burnaby I don't want to be tripping over him."

"I'll tell him. But I can guarantee you won't trip over him, unless it's absolutely necessary. In that case, stand back and let him do his job."

"Fair enough. Just one more thing, and I'll let you catch your plane. Did you make sure that Kelly would meet my pilot at the airport and get Vickie's cat?" he asked.

Something passed through Devon's eyes that looked like irritation. A muscle worked in his jaw. "I told her. I've got a man on standby in case she buries herself in that lab and forgets."

Jace laughed. "Don't trust the absentminded professor, hum?"

"She's your sister." Devon seemed to think that said it all.

"Appearances can be deceiving. You ought to know that better than most."

"*Actions* generally aren't deceiving."

"Where Kelly's concerned, they are. She might appear scatterbrained, but she's on the ball. She's just really shy. Probably comes from graduating college as a young teen. She deals with knowledge and scientific puzzles much better than with people. Once you get to know her, you'll understand."

"I doubt I'll have much call to get to know her since we'll soon be relocating back to Korosol and she'll be staying here."

If Devon's features got any tighter, they'd crack. Jace wondered what the heck his sister had done to rub this guy the wrong way.

"Keep in touch." He jogged around the hood of the dark blue sedan and slid behind the steering wheel.

"What in the world could you possibly find funny in the midst of this cloak-and-dagger stuff?" Vickie asked. "My God, Jace, there's a *gun* in the glove box!"

"Don't worry about that. Devon's just spent too much time in the military. He thinks a man's undressed if he's not carrying a weapon. And I was laughing at his reaction to my sister. He's either scared to death of her, wants to jump her bones, or thinks she needs to be in a padded cell."

Vickie stared at him for a full five seconds. "Well. She's not a woman to inspire fear, and she's certainly not crazy—although those formulas she's always scribbling are a little suspicious. Maybe he *is* attracted to her."

"God help him if he is. Devon tends to be bossy. Kelly might look meek, but that computer brain of hers is light years ahead of most people. She can be a stubborn little spitfire if you get her back up."

Vickie smiled. The distraction was just what she needed, calmed her enough to think about the task ahead of them.

"Do you know how to get to Riverside?"

"Yes. It's about an hour away." He reached over and squeezed her hand. "Try not to worry."

"Easier said than done."

THE SANTA ANA winds blew like a banshee, kicking up dust and coating the horizon with a layer of brown. Tumbleweeds skipped across the road, scattering like twigs as a semi plowed through their path. Cypress, oaks and palm trees swayed this way and that like a gathering of guests at a wedding reception doing the YMCA dance.

Vickie lowered the car's power window, letting in a furnace-like blast of air. The outside temperature reading on the dash said ninety-eight degrees.

After the cold of Seattle, this heat wave in the middle of November felt good.

"You just sucked out all the air-conditioning," Jace commented.

"Sorry. Do you smell those orange trees?" They'd turned down a narrow street in Arlington where acres of orange groves hid both gated estates and seen-better-days houses. That was the thing about California. A million-dollar piece of property could easily share its border with a neglected turn-of-the-century home whose owner thought front yards were used for rusted out car bodies and broken toys.

"I smell dust."

Well, so did she, but she was trying her best to employ this positive energy stuff Jace was always harping on. Her nerves were raw and she had no idea if they were merely on a wild-goose chase.

She was impatient to have this emotional storm over, to get results, while at the same time, she wished they could just turn around and go home.

She'd been watching out the car window, and every young girl she saw with blond hair who looked to be about fourteen had made her heart jump in her throat, made her wonder if that could be her daughter.

She could pass the girl on the street and never know, even teach a class where Andrea was enrolled as a student and never make the connection. Or would she? Would there be an inkling of a bond formed from those nine months she'd carried that child in her womb?

She'd been so very frightened and alone, but even at that young age, she'd known she had a responsibility to the innocent life growing inside her. She'd never missed an appointment at the free clinic, never missed a day taking the huge, hard-to-swallow vitamins that had made her so nauseous.

She'd done everything she knew to do to make sure that baby had the best possible start in life, a chance for a perfect future. Yet the likelihood that there was a child out there who didn't understand the sacrifice, who hated her, was an ache in her heart she couldn't fix.

And in a matter of days, or even minutes, she would know. The terror, dread and soul-deep hope was taking a toll.

"You're working yourself up," Jace said, reaching over to pat her thigh.

"How do you know?"

"Your chest is going up and down faster than Don Henley's drummer."

She frowned, then realized a Don Henley song was playing on the rental car's radio. Raising the window, she plucked at her sweater, which was terribly inappropriate for the weather.

"What are you doing watching my chest when you're supposed to be watching the road."

"I told you. I'm a multitask kind of guy. And you have such a nice chest."

She started to take him to task for staring at her breasts, but the tile address numbers on a birdhouse mailbox caught her eye. "Wait! That's it."

He slammed on the brakes, pulled to the side of the road to let another car pass, then spun the sedan in a head-spinning, illegal U-turn.

Vickie grabbed for the dash. "Good grief. This isn't your Porsche that you can just whip in and out of places. If Mrs. Fennes is watching out the window, she'll lock the doors and call the sheriff, thinking we're maniacs."

"Why don't you let me worry about the driving."

"I'd be happy to if you acted like you knew what you were doing."

Her palms were sweating, and it wasn't from the heat of the Santa Ana winds or the Mad Hatter ride overshooting the drive.

"Take a breath," he advised.

"If I take many more I'll pass out." She messed with her hair, flipped down the visor and checked her reflection in the mirror. She looked like a malnourished waif with dark circles under her eyes. She wasn't wearing any makeup and she'd eaten the gloss off her lips. But there wasn't time to primp because they were sitting in the driveway, in plain view of what looked like the kitchen window.

It was a modest stucco house, with white shutters and gingerbread trim. A grove of orange and avocado trees guarded the side yard. Pretty pots of pansies and geraniums lined the porch, and well-tended flower beds wrapped around the perimeter. The holly berry and bottle brush trees hadn't fared so well in the wind, and red fluff and berries were scattered across grass that had turned brown for the winter. Sparrows flitted after the berries, frightened away when the wind chimes tinkled in the wind.

"Looks like someone's home," Jace said. "The garage is open and a car's there."

"Do we just go up and knock on the door and ask?" They should have put a better plan together.

"I imagine we can start with an introduction and go from there."

"It's been fourteen years. She probably won't remember me."

"We won't know unless we try. Right now, we probably look like we're casing the joint, so I suggest we get out."

She took a breath, gathered her courage. When she got out of the car, it felt like she'd stepped into an oven, the heat immediately sticking her sweater to her skin. She plucked it loose, smoothed her hands over her slacks, and hitched her purse over her shoulder.

Jace moved next to her, put his hand on her back for support, and knocked on the door. Inside, a dog went into a fit of barking.

"Here, now. No need to make such a fuss." It was a woman's voice. A voice right out of Vickie's past.

Hilary Fennes opened the door and smiled politely, holding a squirming poodle in her arm.

She looked the same, Vickie thought. A bit more

gray shot through her dark hair, a few extra pounds, but the sweet compassion in her hazel eyes was the same.

"Mrs. Fennes?"

"Yes?"

"You probably don't remember me. My name is Victoria Meadland. I was a patient in the hospital where you worked—fourteen years ago. In the maternity ward."

"Well, I've had a lot of patients over the years...." It took a moment, then recognition dawned. On the heels of recognition came wary caution.

"This is Jace Carradigne," Vickie said quickly, worried the woman was about to shut the door in their faces. "I know it's rude to show up like this without calling, but it's important. May we come in for a few minutes?"

"Adoptions are final, honey," she said, her voice soft, her hand still gripping the door frame. The little dog with fluffy pom-poms on its cheeks quivered and stared out of velvety brown eyes.

"I know. And I wouldn't be here, but you're my best hope. The little girl I gave birth to might be in danger. If you have any idea how we can get in touch with her parents..." Nerves were trembling in her voice, tears gathering in the back of her throat.

She swallowed, didn't know what else to say, felt desperation fist in her chest and squeeze. "Please."

Hilary reached out, cupped Vickie's cheek, her compassion so innate, and so familiar.

She had done the exact same thing fourteen years

ago when Vickie had prepared to leave the hospital, her arms empty, her belly still swollen from childbirth, tears streaming down her face.

"Come in out of the heat, darlin'."

Chapter Twelve

Hilary closed the door behind them and set the little dog on the floor. It immediately sniffed at Vickie's ankles, yipped and danced in a circle, obviously smelling Sissy's scent on her clothes and annoyed that cat hair had breached its sanctuary.

"Muffin, stop that," Hilary admonished. "Why don't you both sit down. I'll get us a pitcher of tea and we'll talk."

"I'm fine, really."

"Tea would be great," Jace said.

Hilary smiled at him. "That devil wind'll suck the marrow right out of your bones, won't it?"

"Yes, ma'am."

While Hilary went to the kitchen to get refreshments, Muffin jumped on the couch to investigate the strangers. Vickie scooped up the little dog and scratched its ears.

"Looks like you've made a friend for life," Jace said, reaching over to pet the poodle.

"We shouldn't have imposed on her for tea."

"It's not imposing. It's polite company manners to accept what the hostess is offering."

She stroked her fingers through Muffin's curly fur. "Goes to show I'm not as boned up on company manners as you are."

"Don't start building differences between us. There's nothing wrong with your manners."

She looked over at him. "Now, you're not only the ultimate optimist, you're psychic as well?"

He put his hand on her thigh, squeezed. "I'm not the enemy, sweetheart."

She sighed. "I know. I'm sorry. I just feel like such a wretched wreck. She probably thinks we're here because I've had a change of heart after all these years and suddenly want custody of my daughter."

"Then we'll be setting her straight right off, won't we?"

Hilary came back in the room, carrying a tray with a pitcher of iced tea and three glasses already filled.

"Thank you," Vickie said, taking a glass and wrapping a napkin around the bottom so it wouldn't drip. Muffin hopped down and scrambled under the table, popping up on the other side to leap up next to Hilary. So much for the friend for life.

With the dog settled in her lap, Hilary smiled softly. "I don't know why I didn't recognize you immediately," she said. "You lingered in my mind long after you'd left the hospital. How have you been?"

"Good," Vickie said. She wasn't quite sure what to make of the small talk. She'd told this woman that a child could be in danger, yet the retired nurse didn't seem in a hurry to press for details. "After I left the hospital, I contacted the Lees like you suggested, and they gave me a job in their dry cleaners."

Hilary had known Vickie was too proud to apply for welfare and too scared someone would snatch her back to the orphanage. Although her shift had been over, the nurse had stayed late into the night, holding Vickie's hand and listening as she poured out her heart.

"I knew they'd help you out. The Lees are wonderful people. I hear from them occasionally. They sold the business and moved to a little town outside of Las Vegas to be closer to their grandchildren."

The mention of children reminded Vickie of why they were there—not that she could have forgotten for long.

"Mrs. Fennes—"

"Hilary," she said. "I can't drink tea in my own living room and have someone calling me Mrs."

"Hilary. I live in San Diego now, and I work at a nice club in the Gaslamp quarter and I've almost got my degree to be a teacher." Somehow, it seemed important to stress that she was a normal, decent citizen. "Then I met Jace, and he's a prince..." She stopped, took a breath. Well, that blew the "normal" part.

Hilary smiled. "Yes, he appears quite charming."

Jace grinned.

"No, I mean *really* a prince." Vickie sighed. She was obviously distraught and couldn't get her thoughts in order. At this rate, Hilary Fennes was likely to call the cops. "This is ridiculous. I don't know how to tell the story."

Jace patted her knee. "Why don't you let the charming one give it a try."

Hilary laughed, delighted.

Vickie gaped at him. Then she inclined her head. "Give it a shot...Prince Charming," she muttered under her breath.

He chuckled. "You gotta love her. I do—"

"Jace, stick to the story, okay?"

"That's part of it. You see," he said to Hilary. "I saw Vickie across the room and fell in love with her on sight. It took a while to wear her down, but she finally agreed to marry me."

He noticed that the nurse's gaze dipped to the naked finger of her left hand.

"The ring's in my pocket. She gave it back because she thought she was protecting me. I'm determined to convince her to wear it again. Anyway, my great-uncle came to town right after we got engaged. He's sick and desperate to name an heir to succeed him before he dies, and due to various circumstances, I'm next in line to inherit the throne in the country of Korosol. It's a small European kingdom, which has been in existence for over eight hundred years—between France and Spain.

"But it appears there's someone who doesn't want to see that happen. They know they can't get to me, so they've targeted Vickie because she's important to me, and she's vulnerable. They dug into her past and found out about the baby she gave up for adoption, and now they're threatening to make the information public."

"Like a presidential smear campaign," Hilary said, frowning. "Tarnishing your reputation through Victoria?"

"Yes. But that part of it doesn't matter. What's important is the little girl. She's innocent, and this kind of news will go national."

"I've received threatening calls," Vickie said, taking up the story. "Whoever's behind this knows her name. Andrea."

She watched Hilary closely, noted the reaction the other woman couldn't hide. So it wasn't a bluff after all. "That's her name, isn't it?" she asked quietly.

Hilary pulled her lips between her teeth. "What kind of threats?"

"To make the adoption public. Name her. Print embarrassing things about me. The paparazzi will hide in the bushes and snap pictures. They'll hound the family, follow her. And I can't be sure it'll only be the media following her. I've made mistakes—"

"Everybody makes mistakes," Hilary said, waving a dismissive hand. "I've made some doozies myself. And I've done some things that some folks might not consider exactly ethical."

"I don't know if her parents have told her she's adopted, and if they haven't, I don't want her to find out this way. I'd give anything not to have her involved…but right now, my main concern is protecting her. Until this mess is cleared up, I'm worried about her safety. So far, the threat is only exposure, but we don't know who or what we're dealing with, and the possibility of physical danger might exist. Jace has connections. He's willing to surround her with an army if that's what it takes.''

Her fingers shredded the damp napkin clinging to her glass. ''Do you know where Andrea is?''

Hilary nodded slowly.

Vickie's heart leapt. She shouldn't ask. She couldn't stop herself. ''Is she happy?'' she whispered.

''Very.''

She swallowed hard. ''I'm so glad. I'm not asking you to involve her, and I'm not asking to see her,'' she quickly assured. ''We just need to let her parents in on what's happening, prepare them. Let them decide how they want to handle it. Whatever they decide, we'll abide by.''

Hilary set her glass on the tray. ''When I set you up with the private adoption agency, I had a purpose in mind. I had some dear friends who were registered with the agency. They desperately wanted a child, and I had the means to pull some strings. I won't go into the details, you understand, although everything is quite legal and binding.''

''I understand.''

Hilary stood. ''Are you staying close by?''

Vickie looked at Jace. She hadn't thought that far ahead.

''Perhaps you can suggest something?'' he said.

''There's a nice Holiday Inn not far from here. Go out my driveway, turn left, then make a right on the highway. You'll see it on the left about two miles up the road. You can't miss it.''

''We'll be there.'' He handed her his business card. ''This is my cell phone number. It's always on.''

They walked to the door, but before they left, Vickie turned, looked into Hilary's softhearted eyes. ''You were kind to me when I had no one else. I've never forgotten that.''

Once again, Hilary cupped Vickie's cheek.

Just that. No words were necessary.

She felt the years fall away, felt her eyes fill and blinked. ''Thank you,'' she whispered.

''You're welcome, darlin'. I'll call you when I know something. No promises, though. The parents may choose to simply deal with this on their own.''

''That's all I'm asking.''

Outside, the wind was still blowing, the heat dry and scorching. Jace held the car door open for her, pulled the seat belt around her and snapped it in place.

''I can manage.'' She hated to feel weak, hated to be treated as though she were.

''Sure you can.'' He smiled. It was his wicked, sexy smile that deepened his dimples and twinkled in his eyes. ''I just wanted to cop a feel.''

Her mouth opened, closed, then she sputtered a laugh. Which is probably exactly what he'd planned. Lately, she'd been sprouting more tears than a leaky faucet. It was pitiful and demoralizing. Somewhere deep inside was a backbone. She intended to find it again.

She'd need strength for what lay ahead. Jace had

the connections. It was her responsibility to take it from there.

USING HIS business manager's name, Jace got them a room at the hotel and paid in cash. They ate lunch at the hotel café, but Vickie could hardly get the club sandwich down, each bite sitting like a lump of burning coal in her stomach.

After that, they went back to the room to wait, turned on the TV, both of them propped on the bed, the cell phone laying between them. The room came with cable, but they ended up watching soap operas, game shows and Court TV. She'd seen the feature movie before and knew it had a sad ending. Right now, she couldn't face the thought of any more sad endings.

Soon, she'd be facing her own, in full living color. At least as far as she and Jace were concerned. And possibly with regard to her daughter as well. If the girl hated her, she would have to accept it.

To shield their daughter, the parents could well choose to communicate through Hilary, not wanting Vickie to intrude on their privacy. That, too, she would accept.

She didn't actually need direct contact to accomplish her mission.

The ball was in the adoptive parents' court...and the waiting was excruciating.

"Why don't you close your eyes and take a nap?" Jace suggested.

She shook her head. "Too keyed up."

"Come here." He raised his arm and tucked her close to his side.

It felt so right, so good, so warm and safe. She rested her head on his shoulder.

"My mind is running wild with images." The six o'clock evening news was already on, Channel Two's helicopter filming yet another freeway chase that would take people away from their dinner hour, gluing them to their big screens like spectators waiting to catch a glimpse of carnage.

"Do you want to see your daughter?"

"Of course. But I won't. She has a family. I made sure of that. And I have no part in it. I just..."

"What?"

"I can't help but wonder what she looks like. When she was born, the doctor held her up and showed her to me, but she was all wet, her little face scrunched up and crying. I couldn't even tell the color of her hair."

"You didn't hold her?"

"No. Hilary told me I could, but I was too terrified I wouldn't be able to let her go if I touched her. And I knew I couldn't keep her." The freeway chase fizzled out in an anticlimactic ending and the anchorman encouraged folks to stay tuned for the weather report, another subject Californians hung on. The least bit of wind or even the slightest potential of a storm—that usually fizzled out as well—could dominate the airwaves as dramatically as tragedy.

"How do you feel about having more children?" Jace asked.

"If I were married, I'd love to."

She shouldn't have mentioned marriage, knew he was about to remind her that she had a perfectly willing candidate sitting right beside her.

His cell phone rang before she could think of a way to backtrack. The piercing shrill jolted her so bad, she shot straight up off the bed, was standing across the room with her hands clenched in front of her mouth by the time he lifted the phone to his ear and answered.

Her heart pounded against her ribs. She couldn't tell anything from his expression, couldn't decipher from his end of the conversation what was going on. He just kept nodding, saying yes and that he understood. She was ready to snatch the phone away when he swung his legs over the side of the bed, reached for a piece of paper and scribbled something on it.

She moved toward him, watched as he wrote down an address. "If there's a problem, I'll call you back," he said into the receiver. "Otherwise, we'll be there at noon."

Her spirits plummeted. Noon meant tomorrow. She didn't know if her nerves would last.

"Jan and Kent Beck have invited us over. Andrea's at a school play rehearsal tonight, but she wants to meet you."

Vickie's skin turned hot. A rush of white sound roared in her head, pulsing, pulsing, pulsing, and vertigo nearly buckled her knees.

Jace was next to her in two strides, took her by the arms and sat her in a chair. He knelt before her. "You don't have to go, sweetheart. I can handle it on my own. They'll understand."

She shook her head, whispered, "I want to go. But I'm terrified. I've dreamed of this day for fourteen years, tried to put it out of my mind because I knew it could never be real."

He stroked her hair, kissed her forehead. "It's real. She has half day at school tomorrow. The Becks suggested noon because it'll give us a chance to talk privately before she gets home."

THE BECKS lived in an upscale suburb of Los Angeles in a neighborhood where the streets were wide and aged trees shaded manicured lawns and designer driveways. A two-story house with white stucco and used brick accents was protected by a decorative wrought iron security gate that stood open today in anticipation of company.

Vickie tugged at the hem of her white sleeveless sweater, wiped damp palms against her khaki skirt that ended a little above her knees, and glanced down at her sandals. The French manicure on her middle toenail was chipped. It *would* have to be the one with the toe ring. She hadn't expected to be wearing sandals in November, hadn't even expected to be in California.

"You look beautiful," Jace said. "Ready?"

"No."

He smiled and rang the bell beside freshly varnished, oak double entry doors with elegant leaded glass inserts. Westminster chimes echoed an eight note summons.

Vickie had no idea what to expect. Her nerves were raw, her insides trembling. She certainly wasn't prepared for the petite, trim woman who opened the door, took one look at her, and enveloped her in a hug that lasted a good five seconds and seemed to hold a lifetime of gratitude.

After the first stunned instant, Vickie returned the hug, holding just as hard, a silent communication between two mothers who shared a common bond deep in their hearts.

"I'm glad you decided to come." Jan Beck stood back and invited them into the foyer. "Andrea's upstairs. We let her stay home from school figuring she wouldn't be able to concentrate anyway. She's very excited to meet you."

Vickie's heart jumped in her throat. She thought she'd have more time to prepare. Her daughter was just up those curving stairs, perhaps clipping a barrette in her hair and swiping cherry flavor gloss on her lips.

Kent Beck shook hands with Jace, then enveloped Vickie's hand in both of his. "She looks like you."

She wasn't sure how to respond. "I know this is difficult. Please know, I'm not here to upset your family in any way." *Just embroil you in political mud-slinging and potential jeopardy.*

"We know. Hilary told us a little of what's going on."

"Why don't we go in the kitchen," Jan said. "I've put on a fresh pot of coffee. Andrea's a bedbug when she doesn't have to go to school, so she got up late. I heard the blow-dryer turn off a few minutes ago, so she should be along shortly.''

''If this is a problem...''

Jan ushered her into the kitchen. ''We told Andrea she was adopted when she was old enough to understand.'' Her tone was gracious and matter-of-fact, an indication that she was absolutely secure in her position as Andrea's mother.

Vickie didn't think she could manage to be so casual if their roles were reversed.

The house had a warm, welcoming, lived-in feel to it. The kitchen was connected to an open-beam great room boasting an oversize sliding glass door that looked out onto the spacious backyard. A huge sycamore tree stood as a proud focal point, a rope swing hanging from one of its many sturdy branches that shaded the picnic table beneath.

In the cozy great room, a wall of bookcases flanked the floor-to-ceiling fireplace, its shelves crowded with family pictures. Vickie wanted to study the framed memorabilia, to see her daughter's growth captured on the images of photographs taken over the years, but the sound of footsteps pounding on the stairs stopped her.

She went absolutely still. The girl had light brown hair and blue eyes—just like her own. She was tall for her age, with the streamlined body of a young, sleek greyhound. In her arms, she held a floppy-eared puppy.

Vickie had no idea what to do, what to say, how to act. Every thought flew out of her mind.

Andrea gave a tentative smile and moved forward. "Hi."

She wore braces on her teeth. They were clear, meant to disappear against the teeth, but wrapped around them were pink and turquoise rubber bands.

"That's kind of cool," Vickie said, surprised her voice worked since there didn't seem to be any air in her lungs. "Your braces match your top." The hooded T-shirt was white with a pink and turquoise glittery heart resting over young breasts already beginning to develop.

Andrea buried her face in the puppy's fur. "Matches my shoes, too." She raised a foot, showing off pink platform tennis shoes with light green stripes. Her jeans were skin tight, rested low on her hips.

Vickie wanted to advise her on the pitfalls of piercing her navel should she ever decide to do so, but knew it wasn't her place.

"What's your puppy's name?"

"Tinkerbell. I call her Tink."

Vickie smiled, stroked the puppy's huge paws. "Once she grows into these feet don't let her look in the mirror. She might get a complex."

Andrea giggled. "Naw. Inside, she'll always be that beautiful little fairy. I'll teach her that and she'll wear her name with pride."

"She's very lucky to have you."

"Didn't your mom teach you that prettiness is on the inside?"

Vickie's gaze strayed to Jan Beck. What an incredible woman. She shook her head.

"That's too bad," Andrea said. "But you're pretty on the outside, too, so it's okay. Want to go out back with me? I need to let Tink go out and go tink." She giggled at the play on the dog's name. "She did it on Mom's bathroom rug last night, but that was only because I was talking on the phone to my friend Tammy and forgot to let her out."

Vickie looked at Jan and Kent Beck, silently asking their permission first.

"You two go on out," Jan said. "We told Andrea the main purpose of your visit. Jace can fill us in on the details, see if we need to take any action or not."

"Come on," Andrea said, as though she was talking to a girlfriend instead of the woman who'd given her up for adoption. "Mom said we might have to have some security guys around so people can't get in and take pictures of us. Tammy thinks that's cool, kind of like being a rock star's kid, you know? I hope one of the guys looks like Brad Pitt."

Well, so much for worrying about scaring the girl with warnings of potential danger. At fourteen, Vickie would have never felt this sense of safety and security.

The Becks were a true gift. If she'd had the final say in the matter, she couldn't have chosen a more perfect family for her baby.

Andrea led them to the picnic table, letting the puppy loose to sniff at the flower beds and frolic in the grass.

"Tink likes to hide in the daisy bush. She thinks nobody knows she's digging holes and eating the leaves. Do you have a dog?"

"No. I have a cat. She's very spoiled and thinks she owns the house. Her name's Sissy."

"Why'd you name her that?"

"Because I never had a sister and always wanted one."

"Your mom couldn't have any more kids?"

She was obviously thinking about Jan, choosing adoption because she was unable to bear children. "She didn't know what to do with the one she had. She was…" *A drug addict.* "Sick. And she couldn't afford to take care of me."

"So, she gave you up for adoption like you did with me?"

There was no censure in her tone. "Not exactly. I went to an orphanage when I was five."

Andrea looked horrified. "I remember when I was five. I had a birthday party. Dad rented one of those castles that you jump in, kind of like a bouncy raft thing inside. The generator ran out of gas and the thing collapsed right on top of us."

"Good grief."

Andrea giggled. "Dad doesn't cuss, but he did that day. He dived in and held the sides up so we could all get out. Then I said the cuss word when we were cutting the cake. Mom whacked Dad in the arm with the spatula and icing went all over the place." She rested her elbows on the picnic table, flicked her long hair behind her ears.

The gesture was so familiar, so like one of her own, Vickie's insides stilled.

"What was it like for you, having to be in an orphanage—I mean, if it's sad for you, you don't have to tell me." She shrugged. "I just sort of wanted to know about your life, you know? Like who was your father and what happened to your mom and stuff."

Clearly, Andrea couldn't imagine being without loving parents. And that simple fact made up for every single lonely day of Vickie's life.

"I never knew who my father was. My mother was…" She'd used the word sick before. She decided to be honest. "She was an addict, which is really a sickness. I didn't know that at the time. I only knew that we never had any money, and I was hungry and alone most of the time. Then one day, she took me to an orphanage, left me there and never came back."

"That's rotten."

"Under those particular circumstances, yes, it was. And it stuck with me. I grew up in foster families, orphanages and group homes. I ran away when I was sixteen. I thought I knew so much, felt so much older than my years. There was a boy who went with me. In those days, I thought having sex meant that the boy would love me and marry me and stick around forever. It doesn't work that way. Remember that, okay?"

"Mom and me talk about that a lot. I had a boyfriend last year, and when he broke up with me it hurt so bad. He wanted me to…you know. But I was too scared."

"He wanted you to do it at thirteen?" Vickie didn't know why she felt so indignant. The way she'd grown up, most of the girls in the orphanage had lost their virginity much younger. But this was her daughter. Not a throwaway kid.

"Mom said boys will tell you anything to get you to put out. I think she's exaggerating."

"Believe me, kiddo. She's not. A boy told me he loved me, too. But when I told him I was pregnant, imagined we would set up housekeeping and live happily ever after, he bailed."

"That was my father?"

"Yes."

"What happened to him?"

She took a breath. "He was a boy who'd also had a pretty crummy life. He overdosed on drugs. The same way my mom did, I later found out."

"I guess I'm pretty lucky," Andrea said.

"You can't imagine how good that makes me feel to hear you say that. I dreamed of fairy tales when I was young, but when my mom never came back for me, I stopped believing. I wanted more for you. I wanted you to live the fairy tale."

She hesitated. Her voice softened and trembled with emotion. "I loved you. If there's any way I could have kept you and given it to you, I would have. But my greatest fear was that I would make a selfish choice, then end up too young and out of money, with no way to take care of you financially. I didn't have a family to turn to for help. Just like you remember your fifth birthday, I remember that age, too. I couldn't take even the slightest chance that I would fail at providing for you, end up having to give you up in the long run—at an age that you'd remember and feel the scars.''

The puppy came over and sniffed at the leg of the picnic table. ''Thank you for telling me that stuff, Vickie.''

''I just didn't want you to think that I was a bad person. That—that I was doing just fine now and had a great life and had abandoned you. I mean, I am doing fine now.'' She let out a breath. ''I guess I was really afraid you'd hate me.''

''I can't hate somebody I don't know. And I know you now, and I think you're cool. I like knowing you're my other mom.'' She reached for her puppy who'd managed to untie both her shoe laces, and cuddled the dog. ''Jace is cute, you know. Is he really a prince?''

Vickie was still struggling with the lump in her throat over being called a mom. She managed a smile. ''Yes, he's really a prince, and he's cute, and he knows it.''

Andrea giggled. ''Are people supposed to bow or curtsy in front of him?''

''Good grief. I have no idea. Come to think of it, I met the king and I only shook his hand. Suppose I created a horrible faux pas?''

''Did he glower at you out of mean, beady eyes?''

''No, he was quite charming, and his green eyes are very kind.''

''Then I guess you've been spared the beheading.''

Vickie laughed and stood up, wishing they had more time to spend together. ''Do me a favor, kiddo. Don't do any bowing in front of Jace. His ego barely fits through the door anyway—and I mean that in the nicest way possible.''

When they went inside, Andrea gazed over at Jace, her eyes twinkling with mischief. Vickie gave her a don't-you-dare look, and she giggled.

Jace looked from Andrea to Vickie, then winked. "I bet you've been talking about me."

"See what I mean?" Vickie said, and Andrea's laughter pealed.

"What?" Jace asked.

"Vickie said your ego won't fit through the door."

"You weren't supposed to *tell* him."

"That's okay," Jace said to Andrea. "She picks on me all the time. Good thing I'm crazy about her."

Vickie could almost see Andrea's young, innocent heart building a grand romance around Jace's words.

"You guys are cute," she said.

"Yeah, well, us cute guys need to hit the road." He glanced at Vickie and she nodded, then he turned back to Andrea. "If you don't mind, your parents have agreed to let me hire some security people to hang around a bit. It's nothing to be frightened about."

"It's cool. Vickie told me. If you can get Brad Pitt, my friend Tammy will just die. Now if you could manage any of the N'Sync guys, *I'll* die."

Jace laughed. Vickie wished her daughter wouldn't use the word "die." Even in the abstract context.

Jace shook hands with the Becks and there were hugs all around. As they went through the front door and stepped off the porch, Vickie looked back once more, lifted a hand to wave. Jan, Kent and Andrea stood in the doorway of their beautiful home. A beautiful family.

Fourteen years of worry and weight lifted off Vickie's shoulders. She'd done the right thing.

"Vickie?" Andrea called, moving away from her parents but still within hearing. Vickie stopped, meeting her halfway.

"Mom told me you were a special angel. She was right. Some day, when I get married I want you to come—and Jace, too," she included, giving him a sweet smile.

"I have it all planned," she said dreamily. "I don't know who the boy will be, but I want to carry hydrangeas in my bouquet."

"Hydrangeas are my favorite flower," Vickie said. She'd bet money Jace's gaze had just dipped to her back. She was *not* mentioning this tattoo to a fourteen-year-old.

"Oh, mine, too. I'll have blue and purple and pink ones. And I want my mom *and* my dad to walk me down the aisle." She glanced back at her parents who were smiling indulgently, as though this wasn't the first time they'd heard the elaborate plans.

"Then at my reception, I want them to sing that song, 'Did you know you're my hero.'"

Andrea's voice softened, flooded Vickie's heart with such aching, bittersweet joy, the stinging tears behind her eyes, pooled on her bottom lids and spilled over.

"And I want *you* to dance the first dance with me."

"Oh." Vickie tried for a chuckle. It came out more like a sob. This girl was a gem. "It's a date. But do your parents a favor, and finish college before you finalize the wedding plans, okay?''

''That's a long time away not to see you again,'' Andrea commented, scuffing her shoes against the bricks of the driveway.

Vickie twisted the rings on her finger, looked down at Andrea's delicate hands. She'd never thought...

''I have a birthday present for you.''

''You do?''

She removed one of the sapphire rings. ''I bought these after you were born—one for you and one for me. It's our birthstone. I had you two days before my seventeenth birthday. Every day of your life, I've looked at these rings, remembered.'' She handed the ring to Andrea.

''*You* were *my* gift. My gift to you that day, was Jan and Kent Beck, your mom and dad.''

Andrea slid the ring on the middle finger of her right hand, just like Vickie's. Tears brimmed in her blue eyes. ''My parents are the best.'' She sniffed and looked up. ''I hope that doesn't make you feel bad. I mean—''

Vickie reached out and covered her daughter's hand. It was so soft, the fingers so like her own. ''I gave you up because I loved you, Andrea. My fondest wish was for you to have a mother and father who would love you like you deserved to be loved.''

She looked up at the Becks, mouthed the words, ''Thank you.'' Then with her heart full, yet aching, she hugged her daughter, kissed her peach-scented cheek. ''I'm very proud to know you, Andrea Beck.''

Chapter Thirteen

It was late when they got back to San Diego. Vickie's heart leapt when she saw a man sitting in a darkened car across from Jace's condo.

"It's one of Devon's men," Jace said, obviously picking up on her nerves.

"How do you know?"

"Believe me. I've gotten used to these guys tailing me. I can tell the difference."

He parked the rental car next to his Porsche in the garage. He hadn't asked if she wanted to come home with him, and Vickie's emotions were too edgy to put up a fuss.

Besides, she didn't even know if the utilities had been turned back on in her apartment, and she still had to pick up Sissy.

She opened the car door and followed him into the house. The three hour drive from Los Angeles to San Diego had been conducted mostly in silence. Her nerves were frayed and her emotions vacillated between elation and despair.

And then there was Jace. Sitting so close beside her in the car, the stereo on low, his hands so competent on the wheel. Hands that had roamed every inch of her body several weeks ago.

She'd slept in bed with him the previous two nights, but he hadn't pressed her to make love.

A part of her appreciated his restraint, the gentle care he'd taken with her, the support and confidence that had helped her accomplish what she doubted she could have done on her own.

Another part of her yearned.

There were still so many unanswered questions. Coming back to San Diego, knowing the king was still staying about twelve miles across the bay at the Carradigne estate, and that Markus Carradigne or one of his many followers could still be plotting against them, brought the misery and knowledge of what she had to do right to the surface.

Andrea was safe and happy. For the moment.

The experience of the past two weeks, though, left Vickie in an unending swirl of confusion and sadness. Her emotions were raw, her defenses down.

She wanted to stop the world and get off.

At least for tonight. She needed to feel alive. She was suddenly cold inside. Even the glow of finally meeting her daughter couldn't melt the ice freezing her to the bone.

The ache was a constant throb that wouldn't relent. Soon, Jace would be leaving for Korosol. And she wouldn't be going with him.

But she wanted one last dance.

Once more before the stroke of midnight.

Jace was leaning against the kitchen counter, watching her, giving her the space he obviously thought she needed.

She went to him, slid her arms beneath his and pressed her breasts to the solid wall of his chest, the loving heart beneath.

"I don't think I can face another night just sleeping with you. I need…more."

He urged her face up to his, framed it in his hands, gazed down at her for endless moments. "Then let me give you more."

The love shining in his eyes hurt to look at. A love she couldn't accept. It wasn't fair to prolong their parting but her sense of fair play was buried beneath a need that was far too heavy.

His mouth lowered to hers. He kissed her so tenderly she nearly choked on a sob. Then, sliding his hand down her arm, he linked his fingers with hers and led her to his bedroom.

Moonlight spilled through the open shutters of the window, casting several slashes of white light over the headboard of a king-size bed. Ocean waves broke against the shore in a constant rhythm that could easily hypnotize, soothe a weary body to sleep.

Sleep was the last thing on Vickie's mind.

He turned the bedside lamp on low, bathing the room in a glow that evoked images of soft whispers and fervent touches.

With his attention solely on her, without words, he undressed her as though she were a fragile gift.

When he kissed her, his mouth was warm and softer than she'd thought possible for a man's to be. His fingers stroked over the bare skin of her shoulders, her arms, then he slid his palms to the small of her back and drew her in.

With the softest pressure, he took the kiss deeper, without fire or frenzy, but with a seductive heat that was impossible to resist.

"Make love with me," she whispered.

"I am." Jace removed her bra, let it slip to the floor. There was desperation in her words and her touch. He wasn't exactly sure what it stemmed from, and it made him a little uneasy. He vowed to take great care with her.

When she stood so still before him, wearing only her yellow silk panties, he had to remind himself to breathe. He wondered if he could manage the control he knew she needed from him tonight. Sleeping beside her these past two night had been torture.

Now, looking at her, so fine, so *incredibly* perfect, he wanted to take her. Fast and hard. He wanted to slide his hands around the back of her thighs, cup her behind, lift her up and take her right there where they stood, without question or apology or finesse.

He had a hundred fantasies where Victoria was concerned, and no doubts that she'd let him have his way. Heck, their first night together on the boat, she'd broadened *his* horizons, given him a few new experiences even he hadn't considered.

But tonight she didn't need raw sex. She was vulnerable, fragile. She needed tenderness from him, to know that she was cherished. She needed someone to ease her burdens.

And that someone was going to be him.

Oh, he knew she'd built barriers between them, was still building them. He was determined to tear them down.

Gently, he eased her back on the bed, shed his own clothes and joined her. "I don't want to lose you."

Vickie pressed her fingertips to his lips, unable to give him the reassurance he needed. Her throat ached, wouldn't allow words past. With her eyes alone, she begged him. Begged him to give her a lifetime in one short night.

He wrapped her up in his arms, simply held her for long moments. Warm, undemanding hands soon set up a rhythm of touch meant to soothe.

She wanted to crawl inside him, to a place that held only safety and love, to pretend that tomorrow wouldn't dawn, that they could always be together.

The heat from his touch warmed her from the inside out, chasing away the chill that had invaded her on their drive home. Her skin tingled, the sensation spreading like fire throughout her body. She reveled in the heat, and in the man.

The incendiary pull of desire low in her belly made her moan as urgency replaced languor, as frayed emotions receded beneath the onslaught of pure, unadulterated pleasure. She felt her world stop spinning. This was her moment out of time. Only now. Only Jace.

She turned into him, pressed against him, from knees to chest, skin to naked skin, felt the hard length of him against her thigh. She wanted like she'd never wanted in her life, felt greed consume her.

Her lips raced over his face, his neck, nipping and tasting. She couldn't get close enough, couldn't get enough. She wanted him now. Inside. Deep inside where the ached throbbed with the sweetest of sensations.

He captured her hands in his, held her still. For a moment, she didn't understand what had happened. One minute she was ready to eat him alive, and the next, he'd called a halt.

Dazed, she watched as he kissed the center of her palm, eased her back against the mattress.

"Jace?"

"Shh. Tonight is for you, sweetheart. Let me," he whispered. "Just let me."

And she did. He kept his hands easy, but that didn't lessen the impact of the molten pleasure that coiled in her belly, aching for release. She tried to empty her mind, to concentrate on his touch, his scent. He'd been tender with her before. Before didn't even begin to compare.

For what seemed like hours, he gave and gave and gave. And she took. Without guilt or worry.

The pleasure built, so intense she couldn't think. Her legs shifted against the cool sheets. She wanted to beg. At one point, she was sure she *did* beg.

Lamplight shivered over her skin where his lips and hands roamed. He traced every inch of her ultrasensitized body except for the places she wanted him the most.

When his fingers finally relented, circled her, dipped inside, found her hot and wet and wanting, she climaxed before the second thrust. His clever fingers didn't give her a moment's respite. She soared, couldn't catch her breath.

Moaning, panting, delirious with pleasure, she shoved him to his back. "Enough."

She straddled him before he could object, slid her body onto his erection with a force that might have hurt if they hadn't both been so aroused.

He groaned. Or maybe it was the torturous pleasure in her own voice. She felt like this was where she was always meant to be. His body swelled inside her, filled her clear to her soul.

His hands grasped her hips, the veins at his temples standing out. She rocked against him, took them both to the very edge of madness. Desire, urgent and powerful whipped through her, raised chills on her skin, pebbled her nipples.

He covered her breasts with his hands as she rode him, her head back, her heart racing. Nothing existed but the two of them. Right now. Just this. Utter, exquisite, erotic bliss.

Heat built to an inferno that wouldn't be stopped. He reared up, held her still, his arms clamped around her hips as a climax tore through her. The walls of her body pulsed around him, on and on, endless spasms that yanked an exalted cry from her throat. She felt him grow impossibly hotter, impossibly harder. He waited until her pleasure reached its ultimate peak before he allowed his own release.

The experience was so incomparably perfect, she nearly wept. But she couldn't allow the tears to come, *wouldn't* allow them. So she clung to him, held him as though there was no tomorrow.

Knowing that for them, there likely wouldn't be.

"Marry me," he whispered in her ear.

She tightened her arms around him. "Don't."

"Vic—"

She shushed him with her mouth. "No words, tonight, Jace." She thought he'd simply lay her down, tuck her beside him and hold her in sleep.

Astonished, she felt him grow hard inside her once more. She shifted against him, surprised as her own desire heated. Then again, she doubted it would ever truly ebb. Even if she gave it a lifetime. "Just give me this."

When they got to the Carradigne estate the next morning, Vickie had hardly stepped out of the car before she was swept into several pairs of caring arms, passed from one family member to the next like a baton in a relay race.

"We've been so worried," Annie said. "You should have come to us."

"I'm sorry." She wanted to bask in the concern and love, but embarrassment sneaked past her defenses. She'd never had people worrying over her, had hardly considered the possibility. All her life, she'd come and gone without a soul to miss her. Oh, she'd imagined Jace would feel concern, but not his family. "That wasn't my intention. I thought I was protecting Jace."

Annie kissed Vickie's cheek. She could tell by the look on these people's faces that she'd risen in their esteem because she'd been willing to sacrifice for their son and loved one. She hoped that esteem would help them all understand what she still had to do.

Devon Montcalm came into the room, nodded to Vickie and shook hands with Jace. Jace had already called him and updated him on their success in Los Angeles. They'd conferred on the best way to go about security and Devon had agreed to leave it in Jace's capable hands.

On the drive home from L.A., Jace had told her that Kent Beck was an attorney, and felt confident he could put a kink in Krissy Katwell's plans. Kent had accepted Jace's offer of twenty-four hour security until the main players were apprehended. He'd agreed that Andrea was a strong girl, but that he wouldn't like to see her having to explain gossip column articles to her classmates—although he believed, as Jace did, that the whole mess would die down and soon be forgotten like any other political or celebrity to-do.

"I just got in," Devon said, "so I might as well brief everyone at once. Markus has disappeared."

Vickie's shoulders slumped. Jace eased up behind her, offering support.

"I suspect he's hiding out somewhere in Europe. We're working on it. In the meantime, I paid Katwell a visit. Beck didn't waste any time filing an injunction threatening to sue if she uses any of their names. They have valid grounds, because the adoption records were supposed to be sealed."

"Kent Beck is a top-notch attorney," Jace said. "I'm willing to bet Katwell won't keep that syndicated column much longer."

"Maybe. She can always go to another paper, though, so we might not have heard the last of her. I'm pretty sure I've made her nervous. It won't stop her from printing innuendo, but the Becks' names will be omitted. At the moment, she's mostly upset that Markus left without her."

"Did she say that?" Christopher asked, his arm around Annie. "Did she give you *anything?*"

"Oh, yeah," Devon said, a slow smile spreading across his face. It was the first time anyone in the room had seen the handsome man actually smile. It was powerful. Sexy. Vickie glanced at Kelly, noticed the usually reserved scientist's mouth was hanging open.

"I wore a wire just in case she reacted in the typical woman scorned fashion and spilled what she knew." His smile receded, but it left an impact on the occupants of the room—especially Kelly Carradigne, who pushed her glasses back up on her nose, crossed her arms and pretended she hadn't been gaping.

Devon glanced at Easton, softened his voice. "She's not quite to that point yet, but she did slip up. Markus hired men in Africa to plant the bomb under Byron and Sarah's jeep. I now know which trail will give us solid proof."

Easton's eyes turned sad even as anger fisted his hands. Having his suspicions confirmed should have given him a certain amount of closure. It didn't. Easton's first-born son would have made a grand king.

Yet his only son had murdered him—and his mother as well.

"Markus is a bad seed," Easton said quietly. "I've known it for some time now."

"He's unstable," Devon said.

"Yet he's walking around like a sane person." Easton glanced at Jace. "I cannot let him ruin our country."

Standing so close behind her, Vickie felt Jace nod.

"My men will find him, Your Highness," Devon said, then excused himself to make some phone calls.

Vickie berated herself for holding out even a spark of hope that things might have miraculously changed overnight, that they'd arrive to pick up Sissy and find out that the entire world was at peace and there wasn't a soul on earth who felt a speck of conflict.

Nice dream. Ridiculously illogical.

Nothing had changed. Markus was still at large. Eventually, Krissy Katwell would find a way around the injunction Kent Beck had filed, a loophole, print enough recognizable information in her newspaper column to stir up innocent people's lives.

And Devon had said there was no way to know how many followers Markus had. Political zealots were dangerous. If one took a fall, there was always someone else waiting in the wings to take up the banner.

In that case, Jace would still be a target for any nut who disagreed with his politics, wanted to dethrone him.

And if she married him, went with him to Korosol

as he wanted, that made her and Andrea a target as well.

She couldn't put Andrea at risk.

Especially now that she'd met her, held her in her arms, felt the bond that would always exist between mother and daughter.

She twisted the single sapphire ring on her middle finger. Kelly had already put Sissy in her pet carrier, and for once the cat was behaving nicely, not clawing to get out.

"I should go now."

"Don't you dare disappear on me again," Jace said.

She shook her head. "I'll be around. But…it can't be with you."

"Vickie— Damn it. Didn't you hear what Devon said?" His voice raised. From the corner of her eye, she saw Easton and Kelly glance their way. "This isn't going to go on for a lifetime…."

"Won't it? Can you guarantee that, Prince Jace? How many reporters have asked for an interview in the past few weeks?"

Quite a few. He didn't say it with his mouth, but his eyes spoke for him.

"I haven't given any interviews."

"And neither have I," she said pointedly. "Because I wasn't around for them to speculate on. As long as we're not together, no one except Krissy Katwell has any reason to look me up—or any of the people in my past. Use your head instead of your emotions, Jace. You have to start thinking like a king. Just as I gave up Andrea so she could have a better life, *you* have to let *me* go.''

''Vickie—''

''Do you want to see your heritage and an entire country fall apart at the hands of a madman? A murderer?''

''Devon will find him.''

''And who will take Markus's place next?''

She saw the muscle work in his jaw, knew she'd poked at the deeply ingrained sense of duty and integrity that governed his life. The traits that made him so perfect, a man any woman would be proud to love, to hold on to and never let go.

She couldn't be that woman.

''I'm sorry, Jace. Don't make this harder on me than it already is. Please let me go.''

''What about me?''

''You've got a big responsibility ahead of you. It'll take all of your concentration.'' She cupped his cheek, much the same as Hilary Fennes had done to her all those years ago, drew her lips between her teeth and bit hard, holding on by a thread.

''It was a nice dream for someone like me,'' she said softly. ''But I know what it's like to wake up every morning with no guaranteed safety in your world. I can't do that to Andrea.''

''Damn it, Vickie, I know you love me.''

She looked straight into his eyes and lied. ''Not enough.'' She dropped her hand, picked up the cat carrier. ''Take care of yourself, Jace.''

Chapter Fourteen

With what felt like a stake piercing his chest, Jace watched Vickie leave, watched her slide behind the wheel of her car and drive away with his heart.

Not enough.

A part of him understood her reasoning and her fear. He'd be in Korosol and she would be here.

As long as he stayed there, any unrest would be aimed only at him. She would have the safety in her world that she needed so badly. And so would her daughter.

But the part about not loving him stung.

He turned when he heard someone sniff. King Easton and Kelly were standing in the hallway. They'd obviously witnessed the parting.

He hadn't even known they were still there.

He met his sister's eyes. Seven years separated them in age, but they shared a unique bond few siblings could claim.

"She didn't mean that, Jace," Kelly said.

He nodded. He didn't really believe it, either. He

was surprised she'd been able to look him in the eye and lie that way.

It only proved what an impossible situation they'd found themselves in. Still, that didn't make the hurt any less.

Kelly's light green eyes held his, suffered with him, told him she'd move mountains to make it right for him if she could.

And that's when it hit him. He didn't know why it hadn't occurred to him sooner. He'd just automatically accepted that he was the best person for the job.

With his heart singing "hallelujah," he walked over to his sister, lifted her, twirled her around and kissed her full on the lips, knocking her glasses askew.

"Have you lost your mind?"

"No. I think I've found it."

Easton might not have known what to make of Kelly in the beginning, but that wasn't the case now. She was a hero in his eyes. The medicine she'd developed appeared to be working. Despite her warnings about lack of FDA approval, Easton had volunteered to be the first subject in her clinical study. She couldn't guarantee him twenty more years, but the experimental medication bought him more time. Easton felt better, it showed, and he had Kelly to thank for it, couldn't seem to praise her enough.

And Kelly, who usually forgot that there was company present within a few minutes, was taken with the king, as well. Every time Jace had looked around during the weeks Miriam had been training him in royal protocol, Kelly and Easton had been huddled together, talking about Korosol, laughing, clowning and planning. She was coming out of her shell, blossoming.

It was perfect.

He looked at Easton. "Just as you need to protect the country you love, I have to protect the woman I love. I know you're a forward thinking kind of guy, and you and our country will accept either a king or a queen."

Easton nodded, his eyes crinkling at the corners when he realized where Jace was going with this.

His parents had joined the group now, and Kelly was the only one not following the logic.

"Kelly's reputation is spotless. She isn't married or engaged or..." He looked at the king, excitement and impatience growing inside him. "What do you say, Uncle Easton?"

The king nodded. "It is so."

"What's so?" Kelly asked, confusion clouding her eyes.

Jace grinned. "Tap tap, you're it, little sister."

"What?" Comprehension dawned. They didn't call her professor for nothing. "Now wait a minute..."

Laughing, he said, "Gotta go, Queen Kelly. There's a woman who needs convincing I'm her Prince Charming."

IT HAD BEEN three agonizing days since she'd left Jace. Whoever said that time would heal a broken heart ought to be staked out over an ant bed.

Nothing could mend the kind of pain she felt.

Since the new school semester wouldn't start for

another two months, Vickie was lost, having trouble filling the time that dragged by like honey turned to sugar.

She'd scrubbed her apartment so often there wasn't any time for it to get dirty, and Sissy still wasn't speaking to her over that bath episode.

Vickie had scratch marks as a souvenir of the cat's annoyance.

Only the evenings she worked at Diamond Jim's held any salvation for her, helped fill the loneliness—if only for a few hours at a time.

But the reminder of what she couldn't have still ached in her heart. And it wasn't getting any easier to forget with Tiffany and Paul shooting her strange glances all evening, as though they were conspiring against her, planning some sort of forceful intervention to get her into therapy.

In the process of dumping dirty glasses in the tub of soapy water behind the bar, Vickie looked up to see what was causing such a commotion at the door.

Her heart jumped in her throat, settled back down and did a little dance. King Easton walked into the club, his arm linked with Kelly's, an entire entourage of bodyguards trailing them. Devon Montcalm's usually inscrutable features were pulled into a scowl.

A scowl that appeared to be directed at Kelly Carradigne.

Behind them, Annie and Chris Carradigne came in. Vickie's heart pounded so hard she saw stars. With her eyes glued to the door, she waited.

But it remained closed. Jace wasn't with them.

Annie waved and Vickie came out from behind the bar, went over and gave the woman a hug. ''What are you all doing here?''

''We came to hear some good jazz music, maybe do a little dancing.''

''Well, the band's excellent tonight. You won't be disappointed. Can I get everyone something to drink?''

''I believe champagne is in order,'' Easton said, winking down at Kelly. Everyone in the party nodded. ''We're celebrating that *at last,* I've received a positive acceptance in my quest for my heir.''

So, he'd agreed after all.

She shouldn't ask, couldn't stop the words. ''Where is he?''

Warmth seeped through the back of her sweater. A familiar voice spoke just behind her ear, so close she could feel his breath puff against the hair at her temple.

''Right here.''

A broken heart shouldn't be getting this much exercise, she thought. Like Humpty-Dumpty, it was going to crack itself to smithereens.

Hardly daring to breathe, she turned, looked up into the amused green eyes of the man who held every shaky piece of her heart.

Tiffany waltzed up with a tray of champagne. Paul followed with enough glasses to serve the entire bar. Vickie hadn't even turned in the darn order.

Despite the activity around them, she couldn't look away from Jace. He was so close. His eyes dipped to her mouth. She thought he was going to kiss her, right here in front of all the patrons in Diamond Jim's.

Caught in a spell, she swayed toward him like iron filings drawn to a powerful magnet. He smiled slowly, his dimples creasing.

She came to her senses and jerked back.

Reaching around her, deliberately brushing the tip of her breast with his arm, he set an oblong box on the table, accepted two glasses of champagne that Tiffany had poured, and handed one to Vickie.

"I'm working," she objected.

"Lucky for you, I'm the boss," Paul said. "And I say we can all have a drink when it's a celebration."

She'd look like a fool if she refused to join in on the toast.

With unsteady fingers, she accepted the glass, had an urge to just grab the bottle and tip it. She hadn't gotten rip-roaring drunk in a very long time. She decided she was overdue.

And darn it all, somebody had been messing with the thermostat again. She was perspiring like mad.

Jace held up his glass. The rest of the Carradignes did the same.

"To Kelly," Jace said softly. "The new queen of Korosol."

Vickie hadn't been paying close enough attention. The champagne was already in her mouth before it dawned on her what he'd said. She nearly choked, spewed liquid instead.

Right down the front of Jace's shirt.

"Ohmygod." She snatched the towel draped over her shoulder, wiped at his chest.

He put his hand over hers, stopped her.

"Marry me, Vickie."

Someone groaned. It sounded like his father.

"What have you done?" she whispered.

"What I should have done right from the start. I have a full life and thriving business here. You were willing to give up everything for me. I put you in that position, thinking I was the only one who could save the day—or a country. But Kelly's the better choice."

He gently tucked her hair behind her ear, let his fingers linger for an instant. "I can't pursue a life that could ever cause the woman I love heartache or harm."

"What about Kelly? Won't she be just as vulnerable?" Hope was trying to break through the walls she'd so carefully built.

"No. Devon's people are closing in on Markus. It should all be over soon. And Devon will be right there to watch over her."

She glanced at the captain of the Royal Guard, saw that his expression was still stoic.

Jace turned her attention back to him with a gentle finger under her chin. "I love you, Vickie. You're the center of my universe. I can't live without you."

Oh, Lord. He always knew exactly what to say to melt her heart. She'd never been the center of anyone's universe. She'd searched for that perfect love and acceptance everywhere—in the faces of boyfriends, caring employers, whoever showed her kindness. She'd been trying to find comfort from the storm of life, seeking a solace she didn't know how to define.

Now she could define it. It was spelled, *J-A-C-E*.

He took the small, familiar velvet box out of his pocket, removed the eye-popping ring from its nest.

Christopher cleared his throat. "Uh, son?"

Jace frowned at the interruption.

"You might want to remember our father-son chat."

He grinned, and before Vickie's astonished eyes, he dropped to one knee in front of her. She didn't know what to do. A bubble of nervous laughter worked its way up her throat. "Um…you don't have to—"

"You're not laughing at me, are you?"

She sucked in her cheeks. "I don't think so. Did your dad tell you to do this?" They had quite an audience—and a royal one at that.

"Not the knee thing. He advised me on the merits of posing questions rather than statements."

"Did you have a question?" Her heart was really worked up now, but the Humpty-Dumpty thing wasn't a problem anymore.

"Of course I have a question. I haven't followed you all over hell and back and been crouching on my knee for the last few minutes for my health."

Christopher cleared his throat. Annie poked him in the ribs. "He's your son."

Vickie ignored everyone except Jace. "Yes," she said.

"I haven't asked yet."

"Are you going to give me that ring or not?"

"I was trying to be romantic." He yielded as she pulled him to his feet.

"Just the sight of you is romantic. I love you, Jace Carradigne."

"And I love you." He slid the ring on her finger, bent to kiss her lips. Behind them, the entire bar erupted in applause.

"We really need some privacy," Jace said against her mouth. "There's one more thing, though."

"It doesn't involve getting on your knees, does it?"

He gave her a sexy grin. "It could."

Her face flamed. "You're bad." They did indeed need some privacy. Just a look could make her melt like honey.

He removed the lid of the box he'd set on the table, took out a shoe.

Vickie caught her breath.

"I'm still a prince, you know. And that makes you my princess. I looked everywhere for one of these, and this is as close as I could find. I had to have it specially made, otherwise I'd have been right behind you when you walked out on me the other day."

The shoes were silver on the soles and heel, clear on the top with an outline of tiny rhinestones that glittered like diamonds.

"Just like a glass slipper," she said in wonder. On closer inspection she realized those weren't fake chips sparkling in the candlelight. They were the real thing.

Figures. The huge, square-cut diamond sparkled on her finger, and the sapphire hearts on her bracelet tinkled when she moved. The man was a menace when it came to spending money, obviously had no idea of the concept of thrift.

But, oh, how she loved him.

Her eyes filled with tears as he bent down once more, slipped the shoe on her foot.

It was a perfect fit.

Exactly as their love would be for many years to come.

*   *   *   *   *

*Look for Kelly's story
in a special Harlequin collection
available next month
wherever Harlequin books are sold.*

Coming in December from

HARLEQUIN®

AMERICAN *Romance*®

and

Judy Christenberry

RANDALL WEDDING
HAR #950

Cantankerous loner Russ Randall simply didn't need
the aggravation of playing hero to a stranded
Isabella Paloni and her adorable toddler. Yet the
code of honor held by all Randall men wouldn't
allow him to do anything less than protect
this mother and child—even marry Isabella
to secure her future.

**Don't miss this heartwarming addition
to the series**

Brides
for Brothers

Available wherever Harlequin books are sold.

HARLEQUIN®
Makes any time special®

Visit us at www.eHarlequin.com

HARRW

How to Marry A HARDISON

by Kara Lennox

continues this December in

HARLEQUIN®

AMERICAN *Romance*®

SASSY CINDERELLA

After an accident knocked him off his feet,
single dad Jonathan Hardison was forced to hire
a nurse to care for him and his children.
The rugged rancher had expected a sturdy,
mature woman—not Sherry McCormick,
the sassy spitfire who made Jonathan wish
their relationship was less than *professional*....

**First you tempt him.
Then you tame him...
all the way to the altar.**

Don't miss the other titles in this series:

VIXEN IN DISGUISE
August 2002

PLAIN JANE'S PLAN
October 2002

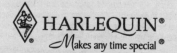

HARLEQUIN®
Makes any time special®

Visit us at www.eHarlequin.com

HARHTMAH3

If you enjoyed what you just read,
then we've got an offer you can't resist!

Take 2 bestselling
love stories FREE!
Plus get a FREE surprise gift!

Clip this page and mail it to Harlequin Reader Service®

IN U.S.A.	**IN CANADA**
3010 Walden Ave.	P.O. Box 609
P.O. Box 1867	Fort Erie, Ontario
Buffalo, N.Y. 14240-1867	L2A 5X3

YES! Please send me 2 free Harlequin American Romance® novels and my free surprise gift. After receiving them, if I don't wish to receive anymore, I can return the shipping statement marked cancel. If I don't cancel, I will receive 4 brand-new novels every month, before they're available in stores! In the U.S.A., bill me at the bargain price of $3.99 plus 25¢ shipping & handling per book and applicable sales tax, if any*. In Canada, bill me at the bargain price of $4.74 plus 25¢ shipping & handling per book and applicable taxes**. That's the complete price and a savings of at least 10% off the cover prices—what a great deal! I understand that accepting the 2 free books and gift places me under no obligation ever to buy any books. I can always return a shipment and cancel at any time. Even if I never buy another book from Harlequin, the 2 free books and gift are mine to keep forever.

154 HDN DNT7
354 HDN DNT9

Name	(PLEASE PRINT)	
Address	Apt.#	
City	State/Prov.	Zip/Postal Code

* Terms and prices subject to change without notice. Sales tax applicable in N.Y.
** Canadian residents will be charged applicable provincial taxes and GST.
  All orders subject to approval. Offer limited to one per household and not valid to current Harlequin American Romance® subscribers.
® are registered trademarks of Harlequin Enterprises Limited.

AMER02   ©2001 Harlequin Enterprises Limited

HARLEQUIN®

AMERICAN *Romance*®

The Deveraux Legacy

Steeped in Southern tradition, the Deveraux family legacy is generations old and about to be put to the test.

Cathy Gillen Thacker
continues her bestselling series with…

THEIR INSTANT BABY
December 2002

When Amy Deveraux agreed to baby-sit her three-month-old godson, moving in with godfather Nick Everton wasn't part of the bargain! Amy never expected that long days and nights of playing house with the playboy would make her long to turn their temporary situation into a permanent happily-ever-after….

Don't miss these other titles in the series:

HER BACHELOR CHALLENGE
September 2002

HIS MARRIAGE BONUS
October 2002

MY SECRET WIFE
November 2002

And look for a special Harlequin single title in April 2003!

Available wherever Harlequin books are sold.

HARLEQUIN®
Makes any time special ®